Imaginary

A Spriggans Tale

Andrew Harry

Dedication

My Dearest Mother,

During the crafting and curation of *Imaginary—A Spriggans Tale*, I have found inspiration in your unwavering love, embraced boundless strength, and sought your endless wisdom. Your support has been the cornerstone of my journey as a writer, driving me to pursue my dreams with passion and conviction.

Within these words, I seek to capture the essence of your resilience, the warmth of your embrace, and the depth of your unwavering belief in me. As I pen each chapter, I am reminded of the invaluable lessons you have imparted to me, shaping me into the person I am today.

This novel is my reflection on your influence on me, a testament to the profound impact you have had on my life. Through the fantastical world of spriggans, I hope to convey the depth of my utmost gratitude and the magnitude of love that resides in my heart for you.

To my guiding light, my pillar of strength, and my source of endless inspiration—this book is dedicated to you, my beloved mother.

With all my love and gratitude,

Andrew

Acknowledgement

I would like to express my deepest gratitude to my family for their unwavering support and encouragement throughout this creative journey. Their love and patience have been my guiding light in bringing *Imaginary—A Spriggans Tale* to life.

I am indebted to my friend, Charles, for his inspiration and camaraderie, which fuelled my creative spirit.

I extend my heartfelt appreciation to my editor for their invaluable feedback and guidance in shaping this novel. Their expertise and dedication elevated the work to new heights. I am thankful to the publishing team for their professionalism and belief in this project.

I also want to acknowledge the readers who delve into the pages of *Imaginary – A Spriggans Tale*. Your curiosity and engagement give purpose to my storytelling. Lastly, I honour the muses and mentors who have influenced and molded my craft. Your wisdom and creativity continue to inspire me.

About the Author

Andrew Harry puts forth his debut novel *Imaginary—A Spriggans Tale*, infusing the poetic essence of music and the compelling art of storytelling, and crafts a unique narrative experience through his enchanting novel that encompasses historical truths of Cornwall and the magic that abounds on the cliffsides.

Comprising 12 songs that function as chapters, the book takes readers on a metaphorical and metaphysical journey of personal growth and transformation. Through the skilled use of metaphors, Harry aptly communicates his and the characters' emotional truths and universal themes that strike a chord with readers as they are common denominators among all who ponder.

The novel intricately and articulately navigates a transformative narrative arc, reflecting the protagonist's journey of self-discovery, awareness, and empowerment, blending realms of music and literature, to offer readers a multi-sensory experience that is both immersive and thought-provoking. *Imaginary—A Spriggans Tale* stands out for its innovative storytelling approach, inviting a broad audience to engage with its profound themes and narrative depth.

Table of Contents

Chapter 8

Chapter 9

Chapter 10

Chapter 11

Chapter 12

Chapter 1

"Song 1 Narrative – Down by The River"

An Introduction

After discovering what I believed to be my perfect home on the outskirts of Lostwithiel, I filled my mind with plans to move there. Here, delightful twisting cobbled streets and appealing houses radiated a serene, historical charm. However, the shadows soon crept in. Days later, I received a call from the estate agent, and my heart sank.

"I'm so sorry to tell you this," the agent said gently, "but another couple has made an offer that exceeds yours."

"What? But I loved it! I thought… I thought I had a chance!" The disappointment washed over me like a cold wave.

"I understand, and it's never easy to hear this," she replied empathetically. "Their offer is quite strong, and the sellers seem keen to accept it."

The River - Lostwithiel possesses a unique charm that captivates the soul. It left an indelible mark on me, stirring deep emotions within. I recall strolling beside the River Fowey, its shimmering waters meandering through lush foliage. An unexplainable attraction drew me to the riverbanks as if an invisible presence was inviting me closer. As I held my timeworn guitar case—its leather aged and steeped in the memories of countless tunes—I became acutely aware of the music within me, longing to break free.

Emotions Stirring Beneath the Surface - Despite my attempts to stifle it beneath the routine of daily life—work, meals, sleep—I found that music would not be silenced. It infiltrated my dreams, transforming the mundane into a rich picture of emotions. The melodies swirling inside me, a blend of yearning and frustration, became too powerful to ignore.

A Serene Encounter - As the sun dipped below the horizon, the sky transformed into a panorama of oranges and purples, filling the air with the aroma of damp earth and wildflowers. I found a moss-covered rock to sit on, my guitar resting in my lap. My fingers hesitated at first to play the strings but soon gained confidence.

Each note I played became a revelation, paying homage to the beauty surrounding me.

Musical Revelations - I wrote about the delicate dance of butterflies and dragonflies shimmering in the golden light. I caught sight of a kingfisher, a flash of blue perched on a branch, its intense gaze penetrating my core, reminiscent of ancient spirits dwelling in this enchanted domain. The river mirrored my song. Its flowing waters carried my music downstream, blending it with the breeze—a symbol of hope.

The Birth of a Song - I could no longer contain the melodies within me. They shaped my purpose and my very existence. I allowed the river to guide my spirit. I wrote and sang, embarking on a transformative journey. I discovered my voice, my freedom - my identity. As the last note faded into the twilight, a wave of peace washed over me. I released the music that I had long bottled up inside. I felt relief gushing out of me, exuding in all directions. At that moment, the significance of my words became clear, and I named my first song, "Down by the River."

Finding Connection Through Music - Each song I create, each note I play, breathes life into my being. The river has become my trusted companion, reflecting my dreams and fears. Through my music, I explore themes of solitude, the exhilaration of newfound love, the pain of loss, the hope in despair, the humility in triumph, the patience in defeat, and the joy in life's simplest moments.

My journey began with a quiet yearning for something greater. I felt trapped in a life that wasn't mine, encased in a narrative I hadn't authored. I drifted through monotonous routines, watching my dreams dim. Eventually, I had conformed to the law of the mundane.

A Therapeutic Outlet - These songs are my therapy, releasing my path to clarity amid the chaos. They serve as a lifeline, connecting me to something beyond myself - a mystical connection to an unexplored realm. More than mere melodies and lyrics, they embody the strength of self-discovery and remind me that hope persists, even in the darkest times.

I filled my notebook with sketches of lyrics and chords, chronicling twelve songs, each devoted to twelve chapters that illustrate a journey I had yet to realise I was on. These songs encapsulate my growth, and the weathered leather cover of the notebook safeguards the stories I've penned.

Transition of Self - Through the world of music, I have transitioned from my past self to the person I always aspired to be—a life filled with purpose, fulfilment, and unwavering confidence.

As I embark on the journey of sharing my odyssey through a collection of songs, I invite you to join me on a path paved with melodies and memories.

The Narrative of Each Song - Each song is a chapter, encapsulating joy, heartache, discovery, and transformation. The first tracks resonate innocence, where the simplicity of life felt boundless. As I delve deeper into this musical story, the tempo shifts to reflect the challenges and heartaches that shaped my character, just as a song takes different melodic lines to reach home – the root.

The Complexity of Experience - These chapters resound with the struggles of love, the pangs of regret, and the bittersweet lessons learned along the way. The lyrics become a liberating release, illustrating how each experience, painful at times, ultimately contributed to my resilience and strength, helping me grow. In these darker moments, where the melodies slow and the chords become haunting, I find the most reflective growth and understanding of myself.

Songs of Hope and Renewal -The latter chapters of my odyssey bring forth songs filled with hope, renewal, and empowerment. With each refrain, I celebrate the triumphs of self-discovery and forging new paths. Here, the rhythms uplift and inspire, embodying the newfound sense of purpose and direction that comes with embracing the complexities of life.

Embracing Transformation - Ultimately, this musical journey is not just about where I have been but also about who I have become - an affirmation of the transformative power of song and the indelible marks left by every experience along the way.

As I turn the final page of this musical chronicle, I am reminded that every chapter, whether light or dark, is an essential part of my odyssey, shaping the narrative that continues to unfold.

Scene 1 - Spriggans

A Sanctuary of Nature - Deep within the heart of the forest lies a hidden grove where spriggans, the enigmatic guardians of nature, dwell in harmony with the ancient trees and wild creatures. The forest is alive with lively greens and dappled sunlight filtering through the thick canopy, creating a mystical patchwork of shadows and textures. This sacred space, with tangled roots and blooming underbrush, is a refuge for us.

The Appearance of the Spriggans - In the heart of the woods, the spriggans emerge—small, enchanting beings that echo the whispers of ancient trees. Our forms, twisted and weathered, barely rise to the height of a human's knee. Spriggans possess an unearthly grace that is as timeless as the forest itself. Our skin, a pale green reminiscent of decaying leaves, blends with our surroundings while our eyes shine with a golden light, flickering like distant stars.

"How come you're so small?" the young child asked, propping herself against a crooked walking staff that had seen better days.

The spriggan, perched among the ferns, tilted its head in curiosity. "Size matters little in the realm of the wild. It is not how large we are but how fiercely we protect what is dear."

"But I wanna be like you! I wish I could run and play in the trees," the child replied, her eyes sparkling with wonder and a touch of sadness.

"There is beauty in strength, as much as there is in gentleness. Just as I stand in defense of the forest, you stand tall even while you lean on your staff," the spriggan replied gently, golden eyes shimmering softly. "You may not always race with the wind, but your spirit dances in the light."

The child knelt, tracing the intricate patterns of the forest floor with a curious finger. "Would the trees feel my dancing, too?"

"They feel all who wander their realm," the spriggan answered, a smile flickering across its lips like sunlight through leaves. "Your heart beats in harmony with the earth. Every step you take, whether on two legs or one staff, sends ripples through the woods. You see, we spriggans emerged from the very shadows of the forest, born from the essence of the wild to serve as its elusive protectors—we are anointed by nature to safeguard the delicate balance of life. And you, dear child, are also a part of that balance."

Relief washed over the child's face, their worries lightening, even as they leaned heavier on their staff. "So, I'm not alone?"

"Never alone," the spriggan assured, a comforting presence in the verdant glade. "The forest watches over you, just as I do. Your heart has the strength of the trees, and just like them, you will grow."

The soft rustle of leaves surrounded them as they sat together in understanding—a spriggan and a child, bound by the timeless spirits of nature, sharing the wisdom that flows through roots and branches. In that moment, the child felt a connection beyond their frailty, a celebration of life that thrived within the forest's embrace.

An Unbreakable Bond - We've lived here for centuries, forging an unbreakable bond with the flora and fauna around us. Our communication transcends the confines of human language; we share secrets with trees, laugh with the birds, and comfort the wounded with a gentle touch, often in ways that humans could never understand. In contrast to human complexity, which harbours intricate thoughts and emotions, we embrace simplicity and clarity of purpose, guided by instinct and an innate understanding of the world around us.

The Protagonist Perspective - I stand just two feet tall, my form a blend of bark and leaf-like skin, mimicking the twisted roots of the ancient trees that shelter me. My pallid green complexion is mottled with darker patches reminiscent of soft moss, while my limbs boast long, agile fingers perfectly crafted for navigating the forest's underbelly. Glimmering with a golden yellow luminescence, my eyes mirror the vibrancy and life that envelop me, catching the light like glistening dew at dawn. A wild crown of dark green hair flows from my head, intertwining with tiny bioluminescent mushrooms that cast a soft, enchanting glow in the dimming light of evening.

Bound to the forest like the roots of a mighty oak, my spirit pulses with the same unyielding vitality that fuels every leaf and creature around me. I often embrace a sense of adventure, driven by an insatiable curiosity that tempts me to wander farther than my kin, exploring the world just beyond the trees. This curiosity blends effortlessly with my sense of duty; I am fiercely protective of my woodland home and all its occupants. Though my stature is small, I embody fierce bravery, championing the weak and defending against the encroaching threats of the outside world.

My thoughts, intricate and rich, often manifest in riddles and metaphors that duplicate the compactness of our forest home. I carry a mischievous sense of humour that brings laughter to my interactions with other woodland creatures, deepening the friendships I share with them. My natural ability to sense the emotions of the plants and animals around me makes me a sought-after confidant, a bridge of understanding between the many forms of life that pulse within our woodland realm.

Wisdom of the Ages - From the beginning, I was steeped in the knowledge of the elders, who spoke of the ancient ways of the spriggans. "Listen closely, young one," my mentor, Elder Aurorah, would say, his gnarled fingers tracing the air as though conversing with invisible spirits. "The trees have stories to tell; if you quiet your mind, you can hear them." I would nod, my heart racing with anticipation, eager to immerse myself in their tales.

As I matured, I embraced the responsibilities of my role as a guardian. "Do you see the balance, Gerran?" Elder Aurorah would often ask, gesturing towards the vibrant ecosystem surrounding us. "Every creature, every leaf, plays a part in this symphony of life." I took these lessons to heart, learning the arts of healing and nurturing.

One morning, I knelt beside an injured songbird, its feathers ruffled and spirit waning. "Don't be afraid, little one," I whispered, cradling it. "We will bring you back to the sky." I could almost hear the winds carrying my words, wrapping around the bird like a protective embrace.

Elder Aurorah watched from a distance, a knowing smile gracing his lips. "Ah, you are learning, Gerran. Breathe life into its spirit and coax the strength to return," he encouraged. "Keep your heart open; the world's whispers will guide you."

With each passing day, I grew in understanding, coaxing life back into sick plants with gentle whispers of encouragement. "You are not alone," I would murmur to a wilting flower, placing my hands around the stem as if to share warmth and vitality. "Let the sun's light find you again."

Elder Aurorah would remind me, "The earth listens, and the universe responds." Together, we forged a path as caretakers and stewards of the wisdom passed down through generations—an unbreakable bond between the spriggans and the land.

The Allure of Humanity - Though I live in a world of wonder, my fascination with humans runs deep. I am fascinated by their thoughts and emotions; I am drawn to the peculiar artefacts they leave behind like breadcrumbs in their wake. While I recognise the potential risks they pose to the sanctity of my home, I also envision a world where our kind could coexist peacefully. On rare occasions, I've dared to emerge from the shadows to observe them, enchanted by their complexities, hidden behind the stout trunks of trees, heart racing with both fear and excitement.

While many of my kin remain wary of the human world, I aspire to forge a bridge of understanding between our kingdoms. Communicating would cultivate a newfound harmony, beneficial to the enchanted forest and human existence. Armed with a belt woven from the strongest vines of my domain, I carry small pouches filled with magical herbs and seeds—tools and tokens for spells of healing and growth.

Each twilight, a sacred moment of stillness, grants me solace with the forest and senses its breath envelop me. My friendships with the animals have gained their respect and trust, enabling me to venture into places where few spriggans dare tread. In these moments, I navigate between worlds of nature and humans, forever seeking unexpected allies.

Contemplation of Life - I perceive myself as an anomaly within the tapestry of life; unlike the silent trees or my fellow spriggans, self-awareness courses through my veins. I contemplate the intricate dance of existence and assert that all living beings experience life on their terms. While trees may lack consciousness, they possess a responsive understanding of the world, adapting and shifting to the whims of the environment. They sense change and react, reflecting a profound wisdom I respect deeply.

The Looming Shadow - As time has progressed, a looming shadow has fallen over our forest. The intrusion of humanity has threatened our homes and the delicate balance we fight to protect. As I witness the devastation of our trees and the displacement of wildlife, an unquenchable sense of duty ignites within my heart—a fire that compels us, the guardians of the forest, to protect our sacred domain at any cost.

Harnessing our gifts, we conjure illusions that terrify intruders, weaving the very essence of our forest into spells that manipulate the paths they tread. Though some humans push onward, dismissing our warnings, we know our resolve must remain steadfast.

The Forest's Last Stand - On a particularly gloomy afternoon, the leaves whispered secrets to the breeze when the clouds hung heavy like an impending storm. Sunlight filtered through the dense canopy, creating a serene, dappled pattern upon the forest floor. This peace, however, was shattered with the distant sound of laughter and the raucous voices of intruders heralding an encroaching danger. A group of loggers, armed with gleaming axes, stormed into the heart of our sanctuary, driven by an insatiable hunger for timber; their intentions were as clear as the sharpness of their tools.

As the vibrations of their approach reached us, a wave of alarm rippled through the trees—a collective shudder, an unspoken language of dismay. The laughter echoed cruelly through the otherwise tranquil ambiance. "What do they think they're doing?" one young sapling trembled, its leaves rustling nervously.

"They're coming for us, for everything we hold dear," replied the wise old oak, its voice resonating like the deep thrum of a drum. "We must act now before it's too late."

"How can we fight back?" a delicate birch quivered. "Their axes are so fierce…"

"We're stronger together," the oak assured, its branches reaching out as if to embrace the very spirit of the forest. "We have ancient magic on our side. We just need to awaken it."

Realising the peril looming ahead, we sprang into action, our hearts heavy with dread. "Send out the call!" I urged. "Let every creature know we must unite!"

The majestic oak—one of the eldest trees in our domain— became the target of their reckless ambition. It felt as if the very essence of the forest held its breath, the tension palpable. "Listen!" I cried. "We need to give voice to our pain!"

"We have no choice but to confront them," another tree echoed in agreement. "It's our only hope."

Emergence of the Guardians - We, the guardians of this arboreal sanctuary, were bound by duty, deeply intertwined with the fate of every living thing within these woods. Our forms, made from leaves and branches, emanated an ancient spiritual energy. "Let them hear our plea!" I commanded, stepping forward to confront the loggers. Our voices rose in haunting harmony, a chorus of nature's despair reverberating through the forest.

However, the intruders remained undaunted, their eyes clouded by unchecked greed. "Look at these foolish trees, thinking they can talk us out of our prize!" one logger jeered, his laughter mocking the sacredness of our home.

"I see nothing but a shadow of the oak to chop down!" another scoffed, swinging his axe with abandon.

"Please, you don't understand the harm you're causing!" I implored, desperation creeping into my voice. But my words fell on deaf ears, drowned out by their jeers and bravado.

With desperation overcoming fear, we summoned the raw power of the forest, awakening ancient magic that had lain dormant for aeons. "Feel the anger of the earth!" the old oak bellowed as the ground trembled beneath our feet.

Suddenly, a colossal guardian emerged from the shadows of the boughs—a magnificent entity formed of vines and foliage, its eyes glowing with an unearthly light. "Who dares to disturb this sacred ground?" it bellowed, a voice that resonated like a haunting symphony.

The Battle for the Forest - The loggers froze, fear flooding through them like ice water. "What the hell is that? A tree monster?" one stammered, voice trembling in disbelief.

"Run! It's just a trick!" another screamed, panic evident in his eyes.

The guardian unleashed a voice that sounded like both an anthem of rage and grief, echoing the desperation of the forest it vowed to protect. With a sweeping motion of its branch-like limbs, it sent the would-be destroyers reeling backwards. Axes shattered like glass, and spirits broke under the weight of their wrongdoings.

"Help! They're everywhere!" a logger cried, staggering as the relentless grip of the forest enclosed him.

"Fight it! Don't give in to fear!" shouted his companion, but no one could withstand the power of nature's sentinel.

The struggle unfolded in a chaotic ballet, the air buzzing with the sound of snapping branches and the uproar of battle—a discordant scream of nature fighting back. The cries of the loggers faded as they were consumed by the very wrath they had awakened.

Aftermath and Vigilance - In the aftermath of the struggle, an eerie silence blanketed the forest, punctuated only by the gentle rustling of leaves as it began to heal. We, the spriggans, re-emerged, our spirits bolstered by our triumph. "We did it!" I exclaimed, pride swelling within me. "The guardian prevailed!"

But the wise old oak warned, "This is just the beginning. We must remain vigilant."

"What happens if they come back?" a frightened sapling asked, trembling in the newfound silence.

"Then we will stand together again," I replied resolutely. "We are the protectors of this realm, and we will not let greed tear us apart."

The tale of the forest guardian became etched into the annals of our history—a chilling cautionary tale of the consequences that follow when humanity dares to trifle with the power of nature.

As custodians of this sanctuary, we stood vigilant, understanding that our connection with each life form around us intertwined our destinies with the rhythm of the wild. We would preserve our forest from immediate threats, nurture its diversity, and honour the ancient magic that flowed through the roots of every tree and the wings of every creature that called this haven home.

A Lasting Legacy - Together, we forged an unbreakable alliance, a pact with nature that resonated with every pulse of the earth. Anyone daring to harm the forest would face our formidable wrath—an unwavering force that was both ethereal and rooted. The trees would ensnare intruders, their roots manipulating the ground, while we harnessed our abilities, using cunning rather than brute strength to confuse and disorient anyone with ill intentions.

Our bond transcended mere protection; we strived towards a harmonious existence, maintaining a delicate balance within the ecosystem. We communicated with woodland creatures through the forest's whispers, ensuring equilibrium in hunting and population levels. The forest flourished, transforming into a vibrant habitat where life thrived in countless forms.

Becoming One with the Forest - As time passed, our identities became laced into the very fabric of the forest. Our appearances fluidly reflected the trees and plants surrounding us, hues of green and brown merging with the shadows. The forest responded to our needs, crafting secret pathways and hidden groves for us to reside—demonstrating our cooperative relationship.

Our connection with nature deepened, embodying a powerful and harmonious force that bound us as we safeguarded one another. The magic and beauty of the natural world continued to thrive, allowing us to flourish as the protectors we were destined to be. We were the forest's guardians, and our unassuming stature represented nature's resilience and unyielding strength—a reminder that even the smallest of beings could wield the power to protect and endure.

A Heart Divided - In my heart, however, I felt different. While my kin observed humanity with distrust and caution, an unquenchable fascination coursed through my body. I saw the potential beneath their clumsy exterior and reckless pursuits; they represented a world of untapped possibilities.

I concealed myself in the shadows, captivated by their everyday lives. Their creativity fuelled my admiration; their architecture soared to the skies while their tools crafted wonders unimaginable to the woodlands. I watched as they experienced the spectrum of human emotions—joy, laughter, sorrow, even despair—and felt a kinship despite the gulf that separated us.

The Urge to Connect - "Stay away from them!" My comrade's voice was sharp, tinged with exasperation. "You know what they're capable of."

I shook my head, my heart pounding with determination. "But don't you see? There's so much we don't understand about them! What if we could learn from each other?"

"They're not like us," he retorted, crossing his arms tightly as if warding off any thoughts of empathy. "They've been our enemies for generations. Why would you think they'd be willing to listen?"

The images of their world danced before my mind's eye, vibrant and full of life but woven with an intricate tapestry of misunderstanding and fear. "Maybe that's exactly why I must try! We've let history dictate our actions for far too long. If I don't bridge this divide, who will?"

My fellow, usually the quiet one, took a step closer. "But what if they don't want peace? What if they reject your overture and—"

"And what if they don't?" I interrupted passion, fuelling my words. "What if this is the start of something new? I can't live with the regret of not trying. Imagine the possibilities!"

"Possibilities?" my comrade scoffed. "Or possibilities of betrayal? We've seen how it ends."

"It doesn't have to be that way," I insisted, feeling the need to convince them burning in my chest. "We fight because we fear. What if understanding dissolves that fear?"

For a moment, silence enveloped us, heavy with the weight of centuries of hostility. "You're gambling with our safety," he finally murmured, his voice softer. "What if you're wrong?"

I stepped forward, yearning for my voice. "What if I'm right? What if I could change everything for us? For both our clans?"

My fellow looked at me, her eyes searching my face. "If you go, you may not come back."

"Then I'll go prepared," I replied, determination etched into my features. "But I won't let the past confine me. The yearning to connect is too strong; I must see for myself."

With that, I turned and looked toward the horizon, the divide between our worlds looming like a chasm, but in its depths, I felt the possibility of a bridge forming—a connection waiting to be kindled.

Scene 2 - My Existence

My existence remains an enigma—a riddle even to myself. I am a spriggan, a spirit formless and elusive, intertwined with the threads of imagination that weave through the fabric of human experience. Like silent sentinels, we have been hidden observers through time, witnessing the rise and fall of empires, the turmoil of wars, and the quiet restoration of peace—all from the periphery of our being. Our presence has lingered in shadows, where the real world overlaps with the realm of dreams.

As I drift through moments, I grapple with fundamental questions that gnaw at my essence: Who am I? What am I? These inquiries have haunted me for as long as I can remember, echoing through the corridors of my mind like a distant melody. Answers remain elusive, shimmering just beyond my reach.

I refer to myself as a spriggan, a manifestation of thoughts that flourish within the fertile soil of human imagination. I have danced beside humanity since the dawn of their creativity, tracing back to when they first etched images on the cool, damp walls of caves or when they meticulously fashioned tools from stone. In those early days, I was merely a whisper—a soft encouragement nudging them toward innovation, urging them to dream and to grow.

Transformation Through Time - As humanity evolved, so did I. The shadows of their dreams began to cradle me, and I became more than a mere echo; I nestled myself deep within their thoughts, meanings, and very souls. I am the embodiment of their imagination, their boundless creativity, and their insatiable thirst for inspiration. Amid this profound connection, I remain distinct—an observer who longs to partake in their extraordinary life.

The Longing for Connection - Throughout the years, I have keenly observed humanity's deep longing for connection, the yearning for something greater than the self. Their aspirations call in the stillness, swirling around me like leaves in the wind. I wonder what it would be like to be human—a fleeting shadow living their emotions, experiencing joy, sorrow, love, and loss in all their intricate beauty.

I have watched them forge bonds, share stories, and build bridges of understanding while I stand at the edge, craving to join in their laughter and tears. I yearn to dive into the rich world of their experiences and witness it through their eyes, every moment brimming with intricacy and grace.

Driven by this longing, I resolve to embark on a journey—not just of discovery but of transformation, a quest to uncover the meaning embedded in the heart of humanity. I know my destination—the essence of belonging—but first, I must grasp the foundation of my existence. Without that essential awareness, my journey will be merely a shadow, forever out of reach.

To navigate this path, I will harness the power of imagination. I will delve into the depths of their emotions and experiences, forging connections that foster a deeper understanding of what it means to be human. This journey will undoubtedly challenge me; the gulf between us is wide, and the nature of humanity is fraught with inconsistencies. Although I am not human, my unwavering determination to grasp my vision fuels my resolve. I believe in the limitless potential of imagination and the power it holds to bridge divides.

A Pilgrimage of Understanding - Though I may never fully become one of them, my quest is one of understanding, a pilgrimage toward uncovering my sense of belonging within their world. I carry with me the hopes, dreams, and whispered thoughts of those who came before, ready to step beyond the edges of my existence and into the realms of humanity.

Song 1 - "Down by The River"

Painted butterflies
beautiful
the breeze
blows beneath their wings

The salmon swims
strong
against
the evening tides

This Is where I want to be
Kingfisher on fire
rainbow
you're perched
in the shadow of the trees

Dragonfly
skimming
your wings beat faster than your heart

Down by the river
I am trouble-free
down by the river
this is where I want to be

Down by the river,
I can hear the song
the melody of nature,
this is where I belong
and this is where I want to be

So, let the world keep turning
I'll stay right here in peace
with the painted butterflies
my heart is full, my soul released

Scene 3 - Painted Butterflies

In this moment of reflective solitude, I inhabit a world that feels immeasurably distant from yours, a realm brimming with enchantment and whispering secrets of existence. I am a spriggan, a being seemingly born of the very essence of nature, intricately bound to the earth and the symphony of the wild.

My days unfurl in serenity as I meander along the riverbanks of Kernow, a landscape enriched with vibrant life and pulsing energy. The air is alive with the melodious songs of birds flitting overhead, their calls harmonising with the gentle creaking of ancient trees that stand sentinel over the land. Each step I take is guided by the soothing rhythm of the flowing waters, my soul resonating like the delicate notes of the forest.

This river is my sanctuary, a haven of calm and beauty that nurtures my spirit. The crystalline water glimmers under the embrace of the golden sunlight, creating a perfect mirror for the painted butterflies fluttering above like living jewels. Their wings catch the light, glittering with iridescent colours—every glance fills me with wonder and awe.

Observing the Wild - A soft breeze swirls around me, carrying the butterflies as they dance and twirl, their delicate movements elegant across the sky. Meanwhile, birds add their melodic voices, crafting a harmonious chorus that enhances the tranquil ambience, making the forest feel akin to a sacred retreat—a place untouched by the chaos of the outside world.

I am not just an observer; I witness the relentless struggle of salmon battling against the currents, their determination visible in each powerful flick of their tails. This unyielding spirit reflects my inner conflicts as I grapple with the desire to venture beyond the comfort of my hidden world.

The Call for Transformation - As twilight descends, the tide rolls in, transforming the river into a canvas of shifting colours. The sky melts into a breathtaking symphony of pinks and purples, casting a magical glow over the water. At this moment, everything feels flawless, as if time has paused to celebrate the beauty of existence itself.

In the heart of this idyllic landscape, I envision my transformation. I dream of becoming like the kingfisher, swiftly cutting through the water, my fiery orange feathers a vivid contrast against the fading light. I long to find solace nestled in the shadows of towering trees, observing a dragonfly as it skims and flits across the river's surface, its wings a transient blur that reflects its quickening heart.

Seeking Refuge - Here, by the river, I seek refuge from the weight of my worries. The flowing water eases my spirit, and a gentle breeze collects my burdens, whisking them away into the ether. As I sit immersed in the surrounding beauty, I am encased by nature's grandeur, revelling in the river's tranquillity that feels like my true home.

But as evening gives way to the serenade of stars, and I close my eyes to inhale the sweet scent of earth and water, there remains a lingering call within me—a quest that beckons beyond this serene landscape. Unlike those who find solace in solitude, I carry an insatiable curiosity for the world outside and a fascination with the complexities of humanity. Their cleverness and capacity for both profound creation and destruction pull me closer to the edge of my fears.

The Fear of the Unknown - I am acutely aware that venturing into the human realm comes with risk. Humans often regard my kind with suspicion, seeing us as guardians and threats to their existence. This fear can lead to conflict—an outcome I dread.

Within me, the questions stir: "Can I truly bridge this gap? Can I navigate the turbulent waters of the human world alone?" Doubts loom like shadows, threatening to overshadow my resolve. Deep down, I realise that to fulfil my potential, I must confront the fears that hold me captive.

The Journey Begins - The thought of stepping into the uncharted territory of human society fills me with trepidation, but the spark of determination ignites within me. I will no longer let fear limit my existence. The world ahead is filled with endless possibilities, and I will brave the unknown to seize them.

Thus begins my journey of self-discovery. With every step I take, I leave the comfort of my hidden world behind, winding through forests and crossing rivers while remaining unseen. I will become an invisible witness, marvelling at the lives shaped by human experiences, their struggles, and the joys reflected in each fleeting moment. Along this path, I will confront my doubts, for it is in this confrontation that I find resilience.

Inspired by the tenacity of the salmon that defies the currents, I resolve to persevere. It is time to shed the shackles of self-doubt and embrace the challenges ahead. I am ready to dive into this intricate mosaic of human life—no longer a mere spectator but an active participant, striving to weave my own story.

A Leap into the Unknown - With resolve coursing through my spirit, I set forth into the unknown, ready to discover my place in this world and unlock the beauty that lies within.

Scene 4 - The Leather Book

As I rest by the gentle riverbank, my thoughts drift like the soft ripples on the water's surface. Suddenly, a curious rustle draws my attention. I turn to see a fox, its amber eyes glimmering with a playful spark, inching closer.

"Hello there," I say with a gentle smile, my hands cradling my prized leather songbook.

"Is that a treasure you've got there?" the fox quips, tilting its head in wonder.

"Indeed, it is. Each song holds a piece of my heart, a melody echoing my emotions and experiences," I reply, leafing through the weathered pages.

The fox narrows its eyes, intrigued. "Twelve songs, you say? Do they all tell stories?"

I nod, meeting its gaze. "They do. Some are filled with laughter, while others… well, they carry a touch of sorrow. But all are woven with the threads of my life."

"Sounds like you've danced with both the sun and the shadows," the fox muses, its whiskers twitching. "Which song is your favourite?"

"That's a difficult choice," I admit, pausing momentarily. "But I think it's the one that reminds me of joy—sunlit afternoons spent with friends, laughter ringing like music in the air."

The fox's ears perk up. "Ah, joy! But tell me, how do you mend your heart when the music turns to melancholy?"

I glance at the river, the soothing sound of water flowing past reflecting my thoughts. "The melodies carry me," I explain. "They comfort me in sorrow and challenge me to grow, helping me heal."

The fox nods appreciatively. "In that case, perhaps we share a common bond with music and nature?"

"Absolutely," I grin, touched by the connection that has formed in this fleeting moment. "Both offer solace and inspire us to appreciate the beauty around us."

As we sit in quiet camaraderie by the riverbank, I realise that in this simple exchange, the worn pages of my songbook, and the rustling leaves above us, I am reminded of the profound wisdom that nature—and perhaps even a fox—can impart.

The River's Voice - Every day, as the sun breaks through, I find solace beside the babbling brook, a stream that sings its melody, blending with the whispers of the wind. In these tranquil spaces, I listen intently as nature's orchestra awakens around me, the gentle rustling of leaves coaxing forth notes that feel like delicate threads weaving into the very fabric of my being.

The Legend Unfolds - Here, amid the symphony of nature, I have encountered whispers of an ancient legend—a tale passed down through generations of spriggans, like me, who have long sought to bridge the enigmatic gap between their world of magic and the realm of humans. The lore tells of a mystical being known as the guardian of melodies who once dwelled here, where the songs of both realms converged. This figure was said to possess the ability to craft a songbook so powerful that it could resonate deeply within the hearts of mortals, granting the ultimate gift of humanity: the capacity to feel and understand love in its purest form.

According to the legend, the guardian created a masterpiece known as the "Scroll of Connection," a text filled with songs that captured the essence of the human experience. Each song was imbued with magical notes that reverberated the joys and sorrows of life, capable of evoking powerful emotions. However, this great treasure was lost during a catastrophic event when the boundary between the two worlds fractured, and the guardian vanished into the ether, leaving fragments of melodies lingering in the wind.

A Spark of Destiny - The core of this legend ignites a fierce spark within me; could my dreams of connection finally bear fruit?

When I first learned of the legendary "Scroll of Connection," it felt like destiny sweeping me into its embrace. With the hope of recreating the guardian's forgotten magic, I ventured into the heart of the ancient forest, taking inspiration from the music around me—the crackling leaves, the bubbling brooks, the jubilant calls of the birds—as I crafted tunes meant to touch human spirits. With each note, the forest became my sanctuary; the ancient sounds reverberated through the towering trees, resonating solely for me, deepening my resolve to weave my essence into this music.

The Path of Creation - Now, the pages of my leather-bound book are filled with twelve songs, each proof of my journey—a beacon shining through moments of darkness and doubt. I share snippets of these creations with the river, the winds, and even the trees, hoping to capture the essence of what was once lost. Although shadows of uncertainty often creep into my thoughts, threatening to dim the brilliance of my passion, I drive them away with fierce determination. My desire burns brighter than any star, urging me forward on this daunting quest for connection and experience for the chance to share my heart's deepest song with the world.

Embracing the Guardian's Legacy - In my pursuit, I often wonder if the same spark that lit the guardian's fire resides within me. With every brush of my feather against these pages, I seek not only to fulfil my yearning for human connection but to become the next guardian—one who brings forth a symphony that binds both realms together, healing the rift that has separated us for far too long.

With each song, I aspire to rekindle the lost magic of the Scroll, believing that through music, I may finally bridge the chasm that divides my world from theirs and awaken something beautiful within the hearts of those I long to know.

The song "Down by The River" - Ultimately, this song embodies the path of self-discovery, merging one's spirit with the natural environment and reminding us that true liberation often arises from a deep connection to the serenity that surrounds us. The river acts as both a destination and a metaphor for life's ongoing currents, creating an emotional sanctuary away from the turmoil of the outside world. In this space, the river symbolises comfort and personal evolution.

Chapter 2

"Song 2 Narrative – I'll Walk This Lonely River"

Memories of That Day

I stood at the top of a hill, gazing down at Lostwithiel, where the River Fowey wound its way through the landscape. It looked like a scene from a fairytale. The town settled by the riverside, its streets and homes aglow in the warm embrace of Cornish sunlight.

The Enchantment of Lostwithiel - Lostwithiel, known affectionately as Lostwydhyel by the locals, is a testament to centuries of history and heritage. Its quaint streets meander alongside the River Fowey, flowing through a town that has witnessed the ebb and flow of epochs, from battles that shaped a nation to the daily lives of those who called this vibrant place home.

As I strolled along the ancient cobblestone paths, I could almost hear the whispers of history carried on the breeze. The clamour of swords from the First English Civil War resonated in my imagination when a Royalist army under Charles I achieved a remarkable victory over Parliamentarian forces at the Battle of Lostwithiel in 1644. The tales of bravery and strife echoed through the ages, and I felt compelled to seek a local's perspective on the rich tapestry of stories that define this town.

I approached a friendly gentleman sitting on a bench outside a quaint café, the sun shining warmly on his weathered face. He was clad in a woollen black and gold sweater, a nod to the chill that often graces Cornwall.

"Excuse me," I began, "could you share some stories or insights about Lostwithiel? It seems to hold so much history."

His eyes twinkled with enthusiasm, and he leaned forward slightly, eager to engage. "Ah, Lostwithiel! It's teeming with history! You know, during the Civil War, this humble little town was a crucial focal point. The Royalists held this place tight, and skirmishes surrounded these very streets. You can almost hear the clang of metal and the shouts of soldiers if you listen closely enough."

I smiled, captivated by his fervour. "That's incredible! And what about the community here? I've learned about the miners and the Methodists. How did they impact the town?"

"Ah, the miners! They were the lifeblood of our community in the 19th century," he continued, his hands animatedly sketching the history in the air. "The Methodist movement took root here, too. It thrived among the miners who sought comfort and community in their faith. Their hymns would fill these valleys, a beautiful harmony echoing off the hills. It's part of what makes Lostwydhyel unique, you see. We have tales of hardship but also of resilience and spirit."

As he spoke, I could picture the miners trudging home after long days of labour, the sounds of their laughter mingling with the verses of hymns wafting through the air, creating a rich auditory landscape of community life.

"What's your favourite part about living here?" I asked, curious.

He chuckled softly, his gaze drifting toward the river. "It has to be the connection to history. You can feel it everywhere—in the buildings, the rivers, even the air. Each corner of Lostwithiel whispers tales of the past. And we're proud to carry on that legacy, to share it with anyone who comes our way."

With that, I thanked the gentleman and continued my exploration, the stories of Lostwithiel echoing in my mind. With its serene beauty and historical significance, this town was more than just a picturesque destination—it was a living narrative, a rich tapestry woven from the experiences of those who had come before, forever intertwining the present with the past.

A Town Rich in History - My adventure began at Fowey Well, a secluded spring set within the rugged expanse of Bodmin Moor. The cool, clear water seemed to shimmer with magic, hinting at the journey ahead. It flowed down from the moors, carving its way through Cornwall's lush landscape, past ancient standing stones and hidden valleys, before arriving in the heart of Lostwithiel.

Exploring the Labyrinth of Lostwithiel - The town is a delightful labyrinth featuring the Duchy Palace, a dramatic hilltop castle, narrow, winding streets lined with independent shops and cosy cafes. As I strolled through the town, I immersed myself in its beauty, the smell of the river, a delightful blend of salt and fresh air mingling with the enticing aromas of fresh dishes being prepared in nearby eateries.

The Old Stone Bridge - The old stone bridge captivated me, dating back to the 13th century. Its arches echoed with the murmurs of the river below. From there, I could see a broad stretch of water reflecting the sky while distant gulls cried their haunting calls.

A Moment of Reflection - Finding a bench overlooking the river, I sat and let the world unfold around me. An angler cast his line. Children played along the water's edge, and a solitary boat drifted downstream. At that moment, I felt a deep connection to the river, the land, and the history of the place. It was a sense of belonging, of being part of something greater than myself, aligned with the ancient spirit of Cornwall.

Farewell to Lostwithiel - As I departed Lostwithiel, my heart brimmed with wonder, memories flowing through me like the gentle current of the Fowey River, its enchantment lingering long after I had said my farewells.

Seeking Treasures Along the River - While walking along the river, I sought treasures, not gold or silver, but moments of tranquillity, wisdom, and glimmers of hope, carried forward by the river's soothing currents.

That day, as I wandered the river's bends, the waters mirrored my thoughts and whispered tales of solitude and longing.

Inspired by the River - With my guitar in hand, I traced the delicate notes of a song. Its melody lit up the emptiness, inspiring me to compose my second song, "I'll Walk This Lonely River."

Song 2 - "I'll Walk This Lonely River"

I'm going to walk this lonely river
each and every bend
searching for treasure
before my journey's end

And I am not afraid of the night
'cause I've got the moon for my light
It will guide me to your door
I won't be alone anymore

I will love you; we'll be together
holding on forever
and then we'll start all over again

Now and then, the river's deep
but it is never still
gaze at our reflection
I guess we always will

We are not as brave as we used to be
but we are strong, and we are free
they will never find our secret place
I will kiss your fragile face

And I will love you, we'll be together
holding on forever
and then we'll start all over again

I will love you; we'll be together,
holding on forever,
and then we'll start all over again.
and then we'll start all over again

Scene 5 - Finding My Emotions

In the ancient forest, where shadows dance with the whispers of the wind, the delicate balance between nature and its enigmatic protectors unfolds. Among the towering trees and the vibrant flora, humans cultivate their emotions, using them as vessels for self-expression and as bridges to connect. These feelings define their existence, moulding their bonds and shaping their societies.

Instincts of the Spriggans - While humans are often driven by their rich emotional palette, spriggans are creatures forged from nature's raw essence. "I remember the last time we encountered humans," said Aurorah, my spriggan mentor, leaning against the ancient oak that marked our territory. "They were arguing, their voices rising with frustration, yet I felt nothing—not a pulse of anger, not a hint of joy. Just an awareness that their emotions wove a complex tapestry I could not grasp." I was a curious young spriggan with a tilted head. "But don't you ever wonder what it feels like?" I asked. Aurorah replied, "No, young one. For us, survival overarches sentiment. Our instincts guide us, and emotions fade like distant echoes. We are receptive to their presence but untouched by their depths."

The Advantage of Detachment - The emotional distance characterising spriggans can occasionally serve as an advantage. "When the winds shift and danger approaches, I react without hesitation," Aurorah continued, recalling a different time. "Remember when the humans built their fire close to the river?" I nodded, eyes wide with the memory. "You just … moved them. No hesitation!" Aurorah smiled faintly. "Precisely. Unburdened by the weight of human emotions, I chose survival, a decision rooted deeply in our instincts. Yet," he added, a note of introspection creeping into his voice, "I often wonder what depth lies in those feelings. We exist while they grapple with joy, sorrow, and love. A spriggan may shed no tear, but it knows how to navigate the storms of existence." I frowned, pondering. "Do we miss out?" I mused. "On connection, on bond?" Aurorah replied thoughtfully, "Perhaps. We see their shadows but remain in the light of our own essence."

Observing the Human Experience - With an apparent emotional vacancy that could easily be mistaken for coldness or calculation, a spriggan grapples with the nuances of our existence. We react not through the lens of human emotion but instinctively, lacking the ability to forge emotional bonds or attachments. As a result, we endure a limited emotional landscape compared to humans.

For example, when encountering a human, my first instinct is not empathy but self-preservation and the imperative of safeguarding the forest. This instinct may lead to confrontation or withdrawal. It is void of understanding of human emotions such as love, joy, anger, or sadness. From our shadowy perch, the spriggan observes this elaborate emotional dance without feeling—a curious paradox.

A Longing for Connection - Although I can mimic human emotional responses, these acts remain hollow, not genuine expressions. I long to dive into the ocean of human emotion—to feel and grasp the intricate complexities that define their existence. I witness their pain and joy but cannot partake; I am detached from the spectrum of human feelings.

My duty as a guardian of the forest and its creatures has been unwavering. A burgeoning desire stirs within me—a yearning for something greater than mere instinctual functionality. I question the essence of my existence. Am I truly alive if I am incapable of feeling? Am I perhaps missing something profound that enriches life itself?

The Allure of Emotions - Amid this existential contemplation, the allure of emotions draws me in like a beacon. I feel the tension of wanting to break free from the comfortable grip of my instinctual reality. I am equally aware of the unknown risks that come with emotional engagement. The contrast between the safety of familiar instincts and the thrilling unknown of emotional experience creates a stormy internal conflict.

A Dance of Feelings - Determined to understand the fleeting nature of emotions, I observe humans more closely. They are a whirlwind of feelings—fleeting, chaotic, and fragile. Watching from the shadows, I find myself entranced by their laughter and tears, captivated by a language he cannot comprehend.

The Storytellers - On one fateful day, I stumbled upon an extraordinary gathering of humans engaged in storytelling. Hidden behind a thicket of trees, I dared to let my curiosity guide me as I peered through the leaves. The scene before me was enchanting: a circle of people, their hands gracefully gliding across sheets of paper, shaping words into vibrant stories that sprang to life with vivid portrayals. Each voice, like an instrument, harmonized with the others, crafting a tapestry of narratives that swept through the air.

A woman in a deep green sweater leaned forward, her voice a soft murmur, "And at that moment, when the sun dipped beneath the horizon, he realised that love was not merely a feeling; it was a place—a sanctuary."

I felt my breath hitch as her words cradled me, pulling me deeper into their world. From my hidden vantage point, I could not see her face, but the passion in her voice painted her delightfully vivid.

"Exactly!" a man with a tousled mane responded enthusiastically. "Like when she first stepped into the garden, every flower a whisper of hope. It awakened something inside her, something she thought she had lost forever."

I leaned against the tree's rough bark, feeling a flutter of resonance stirring within me. Their stories pulled at the threads of emotion I had long ignored, their laughter, trepidation, and yearning unfurling like petals before me.

"What if we explored fear?" a younger participant chimed in, her eyes sparkling with excitement. "Think about that moment when you stand at the edge of the unknown. What does it feel like to leap?"

I could hardly contain my thoughts, an unfamiliar sensation flickering to life within me. I recalled a time when I felt fear—fear of failure, fear of abandonment. The storyteller's words rekindled that long-dormant feeling, not with dread but with an invigorating reminder that vulnerability was just as much a story worth sharing.

"We each have our tales," a woman in a flowy, patterned dress added, her tone reflective. "Every scar, every joy. What if we let our stories intertwine?"

As they spoke, I felt the warmth of their camaraderie wrapping around me, a blanket of shared experiences that made me yearn to join their circle. For the first time, I realised I had overlooked the capacity to feel within me—a different feeling, perhaps, but a feeling nonetheless. Their words opened doors that had long been closed, inviting me to step into the light.

A sense of longing washed over me. I could almost hear myself whispering, "What would my story sound like?" Between the branches, I basked in the glow of the communion, the stories stitching together the fabric of their existence. I was an unseen witness to this beautiful gathering, a mere observer, yet deeply connected to each narrative that danced in the air.

With the sun beginning to set, casting golden hues on the trees around me, I felt a flicker of determination. Maybe I would step out from behind the foliage one day to share my own tale—a story that, much like theirs, awaited its time to come alive.

And perhaps, amidst the shared laughter of the storytellers, I would finally uncover what it means to feel.

Embracing the Emergence of Feelings - Though I lack the physical manifestations of emotion, the tears shed or the unbridled laughter that erupts from joy, emotions flow through me like currents, influencing my thoughts and shaping my actions. This awareness dawns a fire within; embracing and exploring these emerging feelings has become my quest.

Diving deep into his introspection, I attempt to articulate the emotional fabric of my being. I experiment with various forms of expression—crafting abstract patterns in the dirt, composing haunting melodies that echo the rhythm of my heart, and infusing my creations with the beauty I long to understand.

The Strength in Emotions - Through this transformative journey, I discovered that emotions are not a weakness to be shunned but rather a source of strength and creativity. They empower me to connect more profoundly with the world around me, enhancing my appreciation of existence and cultivating a sense of empathy toward the victories and struggles of others.

Just as the humans I have observed conjured beauty through their narratives, stirring deep feelings in their audiences, I also realised I possess this gift. Though I may not create conventional art, I can forge emotions that inspire, uplift, and heal those fortunate to encounter my creations.

A New Role in the Human Experience - My journey takes on new meaning as I come to terms with this revelation. I understand that I am not merely an observer but an active participant in the grand human experience. I will embrace this emotion that allows me to run freely through like an unyielding river, seeking avenues to expressways that resonate with the hearts of others.

The Quest for Union - My exploration does not end there. Compelled by curiosity, I have delved into ancient texts, studied the intricacies of human brains, and recognised a fundamental truth: to experience human emotions, I must merge with a human host—an individual willing to share in this profound union.

However, this quest is fraught with challenges, as scepticism clouds human perceptions of spriggans.

An Unexpected Light - Amidst the uncertainty, I have seen a woman named Lowena, whose spirit reflects an openness that may allow this extraordinary merging of beings.

Into the Heart of the Forest - this narrative unfolds within the heart of the forest and in the possibility of forging a bond that transcends the boundaries of emotion. As I step forward into the unknown, I am filled with a sense of purpose, ready to embrace the complexities that lie ahead. The path may be fraught with danger, yet it beckons me toward an experience that promises to awaken the emotions I so deeply long to share. In merging with Lowena, perhaps, I will finally uncover the true essence of life.

A Solitary Soul - Unlike many of her kindred spirits, who found joy and sustenance in the energy of social gatherings and community-centric affairs, Lowena revelled in the comfort of her own company. She found a unique delight in the tranquil embrace of solitary moments, cherishing the peace that enveloped her whenever she lingered in stillness.

The Sanctuary of Thought - Lowena's mind had been a sanctuary of deep contemplation from a tender age. She sought solace in the pages of novels that whisked her away to distant lands, where she could lose herself in stories far removed from her reality. Music, too, became a refuge, each note resonating within her like a whispered promise of understanding. However, it was the serenity of nature that truly captivated her spirit. The gentle rustling of leaves, the soft chirping of birds, and the subtle changes of the seasons spoke to her in a language only she could comprehend. As she matured, her inclination towards solitude deepened, creating a rift between her and the bustling world around her. Crowds and the insipidness of small talk felt less like social engagement and more like a suffocating fog that blurred her clarity.

Instead, Lowena spent countless hours within the cosy walls of her quaint cottage, where the flickering flames of the fireplace created dancing shadows that complemented her daydreams. She became enchanted by the world of art, losing herself in the strokes of her paintbrush, which translated vibrant scenes from her imagination onto the canvas. The artwork that decorated her home reflected a narrative uniquely hers, exhibiting a rich imagination intertwined with her unwavering attention to detail. Aside from her artistic pursuits, she tended to her flourishing garden, nurturing the plants she loved. The delicate beauty and resilience of every bloom enchanted her. She found an unwavering sense of peace in being their caretaker.

Whispers of the Village - As time passed, whispers of Lowena's reclusive disposition began to ripple through her village. Some townsfolk viewed her as aloof, disconnected from the fabric of communal life, while others regarded her with silent admiration, respecting her independence and boundless self-reliance. To Lowena, their judgments were merely fleeting shadows. She found profound joy in the depths of her own company and remained resolute against the demands of social conformity.

Among those who observed her from afar, I felt a compelling connection to her curious spirit. My heart resonated with kindness and her unwavering fascination with the world around her. For reasons beyond my understanding, I sensed she did not harbour the same trepidation towards my presence as others; Lowena's deep-rooted connection to the spirit realm might render her more receptive to my ethereal intentions.

The Forest's Invitation - I resolved to approach the tranquil beauty of the forest with the ancient trees and the soothing whispers of nature. In this sacred space, I would unveil my true self, share my intentions, and explain the significance of a union between us. I believed we could enhance her bond with the natural world and deepen her ability to communicate with spirits and creatures, amplifying the essence of her identity rather than diminishing it.

A Heart's Hope - Though I felt a flutter of anxiety at the thought of this momentous step, I was equally filled with hope. For what felt like an eternity, I had searched for a willing partner who would understand the gravity of our connection, and I believed with every fibre of my being that Lowena could indeed be that person. I yearned for her to envision the majestic possibilities within our collaboration.

A Moment of Revelation - With a heart brimming with anticipation, I found a place in her much-loved corner of the forest where sunlight filtered through the leaves like golden specks of fairy dust. As I waited, I watched her emerge, a graceful silhouette dancing in the gentle embrace of the sunlight. "Her beauty could stir the very air around us," I thought, spellbound by every elegant movement. Suddenly, she paused, her gaze drifting toward my hidden form. She turned, and the world felt lighter as she bestowed a soft smile that illuminated the space upon it.

Beyond the Veil - "Hello, Lowena," I whispered, allowing the wind to carry my voice. "My name is Gerran, a spriggan, a spirit of the forest. I have long observed you and noticed your remarkable ability to perceive the subtleties that often elude others. What brings you here today?"

Her eyes widened in astonishment as curiosity ignited within her. "Gerran? A spriggan?" she inquired, a mixture of belief and scepticism dancing in her expression. "I must admit, I'm unsure if I should be frightened or fascinated."

I chose to manifest in a form reminiscent of humanity, branches and leaves woven into my being. My gaze was a mosaic of deep greens reflecting the life around us. "There is nothing to fear," I said with a welcoming smile. "I am here as a friend."

A spark of wonder blossomed in Lowena's expression as she ventured closer. "I've always felt an innate connection to the trees and the stories of magical beings inhabiting these woods. I never imagined they could be true until this very moment," she confessed, her eyes shimmering with the thrill of discovery.

"Indeed, you are correct," I replied, gesturing for her to accompany me as we delved deeper into the forest. "This sacred place is brimming with enchantment and marvel. As a protector, I must safeguard its beauty and wisdom."

A Hidden Oasis - After a time, we arrived at a clearing where a mirror-like pond lay cradled at its centre, reflecting the splendour of the world above and the vibrant hues of the flora surrounding it. "It's… breathtaking," she breathed, her voice just above a whisper. I settled onto a weathered tree stump, beckoning her to join me.

As she sat beside me, breathless from the experience, an unspoken understanding formed between us; she was stunned by the magic we had uncovered. "Thank you for revealing this hidden part of the forest to me, Gerran," she said, warmth flooding her voice. "I have never encountered anything like it."

"It is my joy to share the wonders of this place with those who appreciate its gifts," I replied, reaching out my hand. "Lowena, will you take my hand and consider merging our lives?"

Her eyes flickered with uncertainty. "I… I don't know," she stammered, her brow furrowing in thought. "What does it mean to merge our lives?"

Sensing her trepidation, I took a deep breath and looked deeply into her eyes, my heart racing with excitement and apprehension. "I fully understand the magnitude of this decision, but I want to embark on this journey with you. I believe in our potential; I trust that we can cultivate something remarkable together."

As our eyes locked, I discerned the mixture of uncertainty, hope, and an undeniable pull between us. "What if we fail?" she asked softly, tightening her grip around my hand.

"Then we will learn and grow from it," I assured her. "But what if we soar?"

A faint smile illuminated her face. "I believe in us, too," she responded gently. In that heartbeat, a wave of anticipation washed over me, dissolving the trepidation that had clung to my spirit.

A Journey Through Cornish Landscapes - As we meandered along the riverbank, the breathtaking landscape of Cornwall unfolded before us, a living canvas painted by the hand of nature herself. "Look at those colours!" Lowena exclaimed, pointing toward the horizon. "It's like the sun is on fire!"

"Yes," I replied, smiling at her enthusiasm. "Each hue seems to echo the heartbeat of the earth; it shares its secrets with us."

The gentle lapping of the waves against the bank provided a soothing soundtrack, highlighting the sacredness of the moment. "Do you feel that?" Lowena asked, closing her eyes and tilting her face toward the water's rhythm. "It's almost like time is standing still."

"It is indeed," I whispered back, allowing the tranquillity to wash over us. "The world seems to pause in moments like these, reminding us to truly see and feel."

The Essence of Nature - As we walked, the fresh, earthy aroma of the river wafted through the air. "Mmm, do you smell that?" I asked, taking a deep breath. "It's the essence of this magical place."

"The scent is so rich," she noted, her eyes sparkling with delight. "It's like the forest is alive, breathing."

I nodded. "It speaks of life—of growth, renewal, and the impermanence that nature embraces beautifully."

Occasionally, a breeze would sweep through, carrying the salty tang of the distant ocean. "It's as though the land and sea are in a never-ending conversation," Lowena remarked, a thoughtful frown furrowing her brow. "I love how interconnected everything feels."

Timeless Connections - The landscape of Cornwall was not just visually stunning; it elicited a cascade of emotions that rose and swelled within us. "Can you feel it?" I asked, glancing sideways at her radiant expression. "The way the land ties us to those who walked here before?"

"Yes! It's almost overwhelming," she replied, her voice thick with emotion. "Like the stories of their journeys are woven into the soil."

We felt a profound sense of belonging as we basked in the fading sunlight. "Each moment is fleeting, yet so beautiful," I mused aloud. "What keeps this connection alive?"

"It's our memories," she said thoughtfully, looking out over the hills. "And our willingness to embrace both the beauty and the impermanence of life."

In that serene setting, the whispers of the past intertwined with our present, creating a bond that felt as vast as the landscape itself.

Cherishing Each Moment - As the sun dipped lower, casting long shadows across the path, I turned to Lowena, smiling as we walked. "Can you believe we're here? This place feels like a dream," I remarked, admiring Cornwall's rugged coastline and lush landscapes. Each step felt like a gentle caress from the earth itself, inviting us deeper into its embrace.

"It truly is paradise," she responded, her eyes sparkling with admiration for the scenery that surrounded us. "I haven't felt this at peace in ages."

As we continued to wander, I felt the weight of the world lift. "It… it feels like we're part of something grander, doesn't it?" I said, glancing at the sky tinged with hues of orange and pink.

"Absolutely," Lowena agreed, her voice soft. "It's as if nature is whispering its secrets to us."

The Clearing - Eventually, we arrived at a clearing, and I gasped, my breath catching in my throat. "Wow," I whispered, captivated by the sight before us. The pond at its centre shimmered under the sunset, its surface a polished mirror reflecting fiery oranges and soft pinks.

Lowena stood beside me, mesmerized. "It's spectacular," she murmured, stepping closer as if to touch the beauty that surrounded us.

"Let's sit for a moment," I suggested, settling down on a nearby tree stump. "This feels like a moment worth savouring." I patted the spot beside me, inviting her to join.

"I… I can't believe how perfect it is," she replied hesitantly but moved towards me, finally sitting down.

A Moment of Gratitude - "Thank you for sharing this with me, Gerran," she finally said, her voice rich with gratitude and wonder. "I have experienced nothing like it."

"It's my pleasure, Lowena," I replied, feeling warmth swell within me. "I love sharing the wonders of this forest with those who truly appreciate its magic." An idea struck me; I extended my hand towards her. "Will you take my hand and merge with me?"

Her eyes widened slightly, uncertainty flickering in their depths. "I… I don't know," she admitted, a hint of apprehension threading through her words.

The Decision - Taking a deep breath, I locked eyes with her. "I understand it's a big decision," I said gently, "but I want to do this with you. I believe in us and know we can make it work." I felt my heart race in anticipation and excitement.

Lowena hesitated, biting her lip, yet I could see her resolve slowly building. "I want to trust you," she said, squeezing my hand. "But what if…?"

"Let's take it one step at a time," I assured her, gently squeezing her hand as if to reinforce my commitment.

At that moment, a silent understanding passed between us, the unspoken connection sparking a mixture of hope and vulnerability. Her grip tightened around mine, and she whispered with a smile, "I believe in us, too."

Strolling by the Riverbank - Hand in hand, we strolled along the riverbank, the gentle waves lapping at our feet as the sun painted the horizon in vibrant colours. I glanced at Lowena, who paused suddenly, eyes glinting with uncontained excitement.

"I've got something to share with you," she declared, facing me with a sparkle in her gaze.

"What is it?" I asked, curiosity piqued as she knelt by the stones.

The Heart-Shaped Stone - Her fingers sifted through the stones, brushing over the cool surfaces. "Wait, hold on," she murmured, a look of concentration on her face.

With a beaming smile, she finally held up a small, heart-shaped rock. "Look!" she said, its polished edges glistening in the fading light. "I discovered this here years ago and have saved it just for this moment." Her voice softened. "I want you to have it."

"Wow, Lowena," I said, deeply moved by her thoughtful gesture. "This is beautiful. Thank you." Her face beamed with pride and vulnerability as she handed it to me.

"Alright, let us do this. I am ready," she stated, a determined look crossing her features.

Merging Souls - We closed our eyes, drawing inward as we focused on the vibrant connection pulsing between us. "I can feel it," I whispered, opening my mind to the waves of warmth surrounding us.

"Me too," Lowena replied softly. "It's so intense, I… it's incredible."

In that union, I understood her completely—her thoughts, desires, and fears merged with mine. "I never imagined it could feel like this," I confessed, overwhelmed by the depth of our shared experience.

Emotions Shared - Moments later, we gently released our connection and opened our eyes. Tears brimmed as we stared at each other, emotions swirling around us. "What just happened?" I asked, still reeling from the intensity.

In the heart of this lush sanctuary, Lowena shared a knowing smile, affirming the unspoken trust that had blossomed between us.

"I think we've connected on a level most never experience," she whispered.

"I feel the same," I said, realising that nothing could come between us. "We can protect this place together."

Transformation - As the magic in the air thickens, I sense a transformation beginning within Lowena. Her deep connection with nature heightens, allowing her to feel the earth around her.

"Can you feel it?" she whispers, cheeks flushed with excitement. "It's as if the very ground is breathing with me."

"Indeed," I reply, my voice steady. "You're becoming one with it, Lowena. Embrace the gift."

"Thank you, spriggan," she murmurs, her eyes shining. "I promise to wield this gift for good and shield the forest."

A New Beginning - Our bond deepens as our minds intertwine, and a torrent of emotions engulfs me, thrilling and overwhelming.

"What is this… feeling?" I ask, bewildered, as joy floods my consciousness.

"It's life," Lowena responds softly, a smile dancing on her lips. "You're experiencing what it means to be human. Let it wash over you."

I revel in the warmth of sunshine, the joyful echoes of laughter, the deep ache of loss, and the exhilarating rush of love and creativity flowing through a human heart.

"Look around! Everything is alive!" I exclaim.

Lowena's laughter echoes, a sound brimming with understanding. "Yes, every emotion is a thread in the tapestry of our existence."

Embracing Identity - As she fully embraces her identity as a spriggan, I watch in awe as her skin deepens to a rich green, and her fingers morph into slender branches that sway gently in the breeze.

"Do you see this?" she gasps, joy sparkling in her eyes. "I can feel the magic coursing through me!"

"You are beautiful, Lowena," I reply, my heart swelling with pride. "Truly a part of the earth's tapestry."

She senses the leaves atop her head dancing with her magic while her feet anchor into roots that delve deep into the soft, nurturing soil.

"I've always admired spriggans," she exclaims, wonders pouring from her voice. "And now, I am one of them!"

Kinship Among the Spriggans - Lowena perceives others nearby, fellow spriggans, and a warm bond immediately forms with them.

"Look! My kin!" she exclaims, eyes brightening as she moves closer.

"They will welcome you," I reassure her, sensing their warmth. "You're never alone again."

"We shall walk this journey together," she vows, her heart full.

Embracing the Magic Within - Taking a deep breath, she allows her magic to flow freely, feeling it surge through her as the earth responds eagerly.

"I can feel the roots reaching out," she whispers in awe. "It's exhilarating!"

"Let it guide you, Lowena," I encourage, excitement buzzing in my words. "You can summon blossoms and encourage trees to flourish!"

"I can feel the whispers of storms ready to dance at my command!" Her laughter rings out, pure and unrestrained.

A Vow to Protect - Lowena feels a surge of confidence and purpose with this extraordinary gift.

"I vow to safeguard the forest and all its inhabitants from harm," she declares, a fierce light in her eyes. "I promise to heal the land!"

"And I shall assist you," I vow back, feeling the depth of our connection. "Together, we will ensure its fertility for generations to come."

The Essence of Humanity - Amidst this transformation, Lowena's human essence remains integral to her identity.

"I carry my memories with me," she reflects, a thoughtful expression crossing her face. "Each joy and sorrow shapes who I am."

"It enriches you, Lowena," I affirm. "Your humanity is forever a part of your spirit."

Embracing Human Emotions - Lowena will guide me to embrace the entirety of human emotions—whether joy, sorrow, anger, or fear.

"You will learn alongside me," she promises, taking my hand gently. "Every feeling is essential to truly living."

"Together, we can face it all," I assure her, feeling a newfound determination. "We will cry when sadness engulfs us and laugh when joy envelops us."

"And express our frustrations freely," she adds with a grin.

A Sacred Bond - We forge a bond rooted in hope and love in this sacred place.

"This connection is powerful," Lowena says softly, drawing closer. "Our shared purpose fuels this magic."

"We protect one another and the world around us," I conclude, resonating with her sentiment.

Together, we become a part of the forest, its secrets whispering through the trees as we embrace our intertwined destinies.

"Let the magic guide us," Lowena breathes, her gaze searching the horizon. "Together, we are unstoppable."

Scene 6 - Drinking From The River

The Call of the River - Our next move is to drink from the river, a shimmering ribbon of life that weaves its way through the heart of this landscape. It promises to be our vital source, grounding us firmly in the earth's embrace and reconnecting us to the natural world.

The First Sip - I kneel at the riverbank and take my first sip; an immediate shift envelops me. A wave of energy surges through my veins—it's as if an enchanting force has awakened something deep within, restoring every part of my being with each refreshing gulp. The water is the essence of the earth itself. With every drop that trickles down my throat, I feel my spirit revitalising, nourished by this pure tonic of life. It ignites a spark of creativity, clearing the fog from my mind like a reboot of forgotten dreams. Suddenly, clarity washes over me, and I become aware of a newfound sense of direction.

Guided by the Flow - With each sip, I feel myself being transported beyond the physical world into realms of possibility. The river acts as my compass, guiding me through this unfamiliar territory with its gentle flow. A deeper swallow sends a cool breeze spiralling from a distance, caressing my skin and invigorating my senses. At that moment, I realised this is where my journey begins—this is our beginning, Lowena's and mine.

Embracing the Surroundings - I stretch my arms toward the sun, relishing the warmth that envelops my fingertips. My senses heighten as I begin to absorb the beauty that surrounds me. The portals of my soul fly wide open; I can see, smell, hear, and taste everything with astonishing clarity. The aromas swirling around me are unlike anything I have ever encountered, a harmonious blend of sweetness, saltiness, and bitter earth that dances on my palate. It feels simultaneously surreal and entirely natural. I am in awe, intoxicated by the vibrant world that springs to life under my newfound perception.

A Cocoon of Serenity - Sitting beside the river, I am enveloped in a cocoon of peace and serenity. The burdens of my worries and fears are lifted, and in their place, I feel a sense of liberation—it's as though I have been reborn. The sun wraps around me from every angle, and within, a sense of infinity unfurls like petals in bloom. Is this love? The overwhelming feeling stirs within me, igniting existential questions about the very essence of life itself.

The Dawn of Change - I can feel the transformation within as I drink from the river. I stand on the brink of change, aware that this moment marks the beginning of an extraordinary adventure. Glancing toward Lowena, I feel a deep sense of connection and curiosity: who knows what awaits us on this journey? But one certainty anchors me to this riverbank— I long to embrace everything the future holds. With renewed courage, I am ready to embark on this new beginning, fully prepared to navigate whatever lies ahead.

Scene 7 - The Winding River of Life

The Journey Begins - The river of life continues with a graceful unpredictability, its path twisting and turning through landscapes familiar and foreign. Each bend brings new experiences, challenges, and revelations. For as long as I can remember, I have embarked on this winding journey, uncertain where it might lead. As I take the first steps onto the riverbank, a sense of anticipation stirs within me—what treasures might be waiting to be discovered along this watery trail?

A Glimmering Surface - The sun casts a shimmering glow upon the surface, transforming its gentle ripples into a spectacle of light. I can't help but be captivated by its beauty, for the river feels like a precious gift—an eternal source of wisdom. As I peer into its clear depths, I am drawn to small glimmers that twinkle beneath the surface. Are these the treasures I've sought with such passion? Upon closer inspection, I realise these aren't mere ordinary pieces of gold; they are something far more profound. Each nugget bears a word, a phrase, or a symbol—fragments of greater truths, each promising to illuminate my path and guide my journey forward. Their presence fills me with gratitude and clarity, as if the river acknowledges my quest for understanding.

Navigating the Unknown - As I negotiate the riverbanks, the sun beats down on my back while the current gently resists my progress. This river has guided me through countless chapters of my life, steering me from the comforting shores of familiarity into the murky waters of the unknown. I have come to believe that it's the key to unlocking my true potential. "Perhaps the river has even more in store for me," I ponder, my thoughts reverberating softly through the lush foliage lining the banks.

Navigating the Unknown - A flash of brilliant sunlight catches my eye as I delve deeper into my reflections. In the muddy bank etched deeply into the earth, I discover a series of numbers; they are coordinates. My heart quickens with anticipation. Though I have rarely considered myself a follower of fate or destiny, the river seems to be revealing a secret just for me, beckoning me toward something significant.

Following the Path - Driven by a newfound resolve, I set out to follow the coordinates, weaving gracefully through the river's curves as its depths gradually increase. After an eternity of navigating hidden paths and rippling waves, I finally arrive at a small island shrouded in mystery. It lies tangled in vines and enshrouded by an eerie mist, as if nature is purposely concealing its secrets from the world.

A Hidden Sanctuary - Stepping onto the moss-covered shore, I am swept away by the sensory wonders that greet me. The air is rich with earthy scents, wildflowers sway gently in the breeze, and the melodic sound of birdsong fills my heart with a profound sense of calm. This island feels pristine, almost like a sanctuary—a haven offering respite from the chaos of life.

Unveiling the Treasure - As I explore further, I discover a clearing nestled among the ancient trees, illuminated by a warm, golden glow. At the centre stands a magnificent tree, its branches stretching skyward like a pair of welcoming arms. Beneath its vast canopy lies a small wooden chest, its surface glimmering in the sunlight. Curiosity tinged with excitement urges me forward.

A Lesson from the Scrolls - I gently unroll the Scroll of Connection, its ancient parchment crackling softly in the stillness. The words seem to shimmer with a life of their own, beckoning me closer.

"Elder Aurorah," I whisper, feeling his wise presence beside me as if he is guiding me again. "What do these teachings mean for someone like me, who has wandered so aimlessly?"

His warm and melodic voice flows through the air like a gentle breeze. "Ah, my dear Gerran, the journey to enlightenment often begins with recognising one's restlessness. Understand that what you seek is not treasure, but the understanding of connection—the invisible threads that tie us to one another and the world around us.”

“But how can I change the pattern of my past?” I ask, recalling those moments of conflict and disconnection. “So often, I dismissed others or hardened my heart against their struggles.”

Elder Aurorah chuckles softly, his laughter like the sound of leaves rustling. “Change is like the rhythm of the tides, my young dreamer. With every wave that ebbs, a new one flows in. Each experience is but a stroke on the canvas of your life. Embrace it, and see the beauty in your imperfections.”

I nod, feeling a weight lift as I immerse myself in his wisdom. “And these indigenous teachings speak of harmony with nature… I’ve often felt so disconnected from it all, lost in the chaos of modern life.”

“Nature is a mirror, reflecting your innermost state,” Elder Aurorah replies, his eyes sparkling like stars. “To harmonize with it, you must first harmonize within yourself. Listen to the whispers of the wind and the songs of the rivers. They hold the key to understanding your place in this vast tapestry of existence.”

I close my eyes, envisioning the breathtaking landscapes I had only superficially admired. “If every action creates ripples, then what can I do to create ripples of kindness rather than strife?”

"Ah, that is the essence of transformation! Kindness is not a mere act but a way of being," he intones, his voice resonating in my heart. "Let empathy guide your steps. When you listen to others and recognize their struggles and joys, you create ripples of understanding that can traverse the oceans of indifference."

"But I feel so small in this vast world," I confess, my voice barely above a whisper. "Can one person really make a difference?"

Elder Aurorah's gaze is steady, his wisdom unwavering. "Every great journey begins with a single step. Just as a small stone can create ripples that spread far beyond its point of entry, so too can your acts of kindness resonate within the hearts of many. Be the change you wish to see, and let your heart be the compass that guides you."

As I absorb his words, a sense of clarity washes over me—a realization that the scrolls are not just texts to be read but living lessons to be embodied. "Thank you, Elder Aurorah. I see now that true enrichment comes not from the treasures we possess but from the connections we nurture."

With a smile, he watches as I take a deep breath, the wisdom of the ages infusing my spirit. "Now go forth, my student. Let the lessons of the scrolls echo in your actions, and may you weave a tapestry of connection, understanding, and love that transcends time itself."

A New Purpose - This enlightened understanding has opened my eyes to the beauty surrounding me. The scroll weaves together the messages of love, compassion, and responsibility, igniting a fire within me that I never knew existed. I now see how my purpose is to be a conduit of this wisdom, to spread the knowledge I have gained to others, fostering unity and understanding in a world divided.

A Richness Beyond Measure - As I turn to leave the island, a sense of peace envelops me. I may not have a treasure chest overflowing with material riches, but I am rich beyond measure. I carry with me the essence of every scroll, the heartbeats of wisdom captured in their folds, and the knowledge that my life's journey will be one of connection, empathy, and transformation.

The Awakening - The river has indeed led me to true treasure—an awakening to my genuine self and the calling that awaits me beyond the horizon. I realise that my journey, fuelled by the timeless truths of the ancients, has only just begun, and I am ready to take the first step. As I leave the island, I may not carry a treasure chest filled with jewels, but I walk away with a heart overflowing with knowledge and a soul brimming with purpose. The river, my silent guide, has unveiled a hidden truth that will forever alter the course of my life. I discover that true wealth lies not in material possessions but in the boundless potential within me.

Fresh Perspectives - Every moment from that day forward is infused with renewed clarity and direction. I visualise my path extending before me, each twist and turn revealing opportunities for growth. As the river widens and its current slows, I will be nearing the conclusion of this chapter of my journey. When the river flows into a vast lake or perhaps an ocean, I will rise stronger and wiser, firmly grounded when my feet finally touch solid ground.

The Transformation - At that moment, I will better understand who I have become and how far I have travelled. This journey is undeniably mine—a transformative odyssey more beautiful and fulfilling than I ever dared to dream possible.

The song "I'll Walk This Lonely River" captures a journey of love, resilience, and self-discovery. The protagonist embarks on a symbolic trek down a winding river, symbolising the twists and turns of life and relationships. The imagery of a "lonely river" evokes feelings of solitude, yet it is contrasted with the comforting presence of the moonlight, representing hope and guidance through dark times. This duality mirrors the human experience of navigation through isolation while seeking connection.

Ultimately, the reiteration of beginning anew encapsulates the cycle of love, loss, and rebirth, suggesting that every journey, no matter how lonely, holds the potential for rediscovery and rejuvenation. The song serves as a heartfelt reminder that through the ebb and flow of life's river, love persists, guiding us back to connection and new beginnings.

Chapter 3

"Song 3 Narrative – My Lovely Lady"

A Song to Reflect the Seasons

Composing the third song, "My Lovely Lady," came effortlessly, almost like an epiphany. Strolling beneath the trees that flanked the riverbanks, Fowey felt like wandering through an enchanted woodland, where vibrant emerald leaves whispered their secrets and flowers swayed gently in the breeze. I envisioned a song that captured the essence of the changing seasons, inspired by a breathtaking Cornish maiden who enchanted all who laid eyes on her.

The Enchanted Maiden - With eyes that shimmered like fresh leaves of spring, she possessed a gaze capable of summoning slumbering souls. Her hair was a flowing cascade of fiery red, draping like silk over her delicate shoulders, and her face was one of nature's marvels, with contours as soft as petals and features reminiscent of a forest nymph.

The Legend of Her Beauty - Her beauty was a part of legends and was said to have inspired tales throughout the land. It was believed that the seasons themselves paid tribute to her beauty.

The Awakening - she donned the freshest leaves and sweetest blooms, her eyes sparkling with the vitality of new beginnings while her hair glistened in the golden light.

A Kaleidoscope of Colours - As summer embraced her, a kaleidoscope of colours emerged. Her hair transformed into a rich blend of red and orange, echoing the ripening berries and the first hints of autumn. Her eyes radiated warmth, basking in the golden tones of sunset that enveloped the forest.

The Wisdom of Change - When autumn arrived, it draped her in a cloak of russet and amber, her eyes reflecting the wisdom of fallen leaves while her hair captured the soft light of the fading season.

A Shimmering Halo - Winter, too, left its mark, laying a delicate frost upon her. Her hair became a shimmering halo of silver, and her eyes sparkled with the mesmerising brilliance of snowflakes.

An Enduring Tribute - Her beauty remained a constant throughout the shifting seasons, a reminder of nature's enduring artistry. The song "My Lovely Lady" echoed through the forest, a timeless tribute to her extraordinary grace and the harmonious relationship she shared with the world around her

Song 3 - "My Lovely Lady"

The greenest eyes, the reddest hair
The prettiest face anywhere
Beauty beyond compare
my lovely lady

Dance beneath the Cornish moon
daylight comes all too soon
Solstice in the month of June
my lovely lady

Hold my hand; don't let go
No, no, no, no, no, no
my lovely lady

Making love on the meadow ground
Mother Nature all around
Leave this place as it was found
Oh, my lovely lady
Hold my hand; don't let go
No, no, no no, no, no
my lovely lady

The greenest eyes, the reddest hair
The prettiest face anywhere
Beauty beyond compare, my lovely lady

Scene 8 - My Reflection

A Moment by the River - The river flows deep beneath a facade of stillness and calmness from my vantage point on the bank. As the sun sets, it bathes the water in a golden glow. Yet, as I watch the river's surface, an unsettling feeling overcomes me, a sense of danger, as though the river beckons me, enticing me to its edge. Compelled by an irresistible urge, I step closer, yearning to touch the water. This longing feels urgent.

The Touch of Water - When my fingers meet its surface, a chill radiates through me—almost icy, invigorating. It feels as if the water carries whispers from a distant past, but at this moment, I am untroubled. This feels destined. My fingertips disturb the water, and ripples dance outwards, forming hypnotic patterns that fade into stillness. I cannot watch. I must dive deeper into the mysteries that this river holds. With each step I take, warmth envelops me, a blend of calm and thrilling anticipation of something wonderful to unravel.

A Revelation in Reflection - I see it myself in the reflective water. It's a revelation, an emergence. I have always wondered what I would look like in human form, but witnessing my reflection is a new experience. Surprisingly, I am not critical of my appearance. Instead, this reflection reveals aspects of my emotional being as well. I realize I must acknowledge and harness these newfound emotions. Without hesitation, I reach out to touch the earth, then my face, leaving a mark that connects me to this moment.

Acceptance of Self - Glance at my reflection again, unable to look away for even a second. I first notice my hair, a tangled mass of reddish- brown, and my eyes shimmering with curiosity and wonder. My skin carries a muted yellow hue, and my large, pointed ears echo the sleekness of a hawk. My nose, sharp and beak-like, complements my thin lips. As I drink in these features, a wave of acceptance and kindness swells within me. I approached my reflection with compassion, letting go of disapproval and nerves. It works. A sense of peace washes over me as I contemplate the person staring back. This is me, and I am ready to embrace my true self.

Transformation Begins - With newfound confidence, I step back from the river, aware that this experience has changed me. I have faced my fears and accepted my accurate reflection, one I can now welcome. For the first time, I feel aware of my surroundings. No longer a tentative child, I am a brave adventurer who has discovered treasure within. The emotions and experiences of humanity pulse through me, filling me with wonder. As I glance at my hands, almost human, I realize my transformation is nearly complete.

The Encounter with Lowena - And then, I see her. Her eyes gleam like emeralds, mirroring the vibrant greens of the forest, as if concealing secrets only the wild understands. Lowena's hair flows like a fiery auburn-haired waterfall, dancing in the breeze, casting an alluring glow across her delicate features. Her skin is as luminous as morning dew, and her lips bear the colour of ripe berries—a vision of stunning beauty. She captivates all the forest creatures.

The Whisper of the Forest - As the summer solstice nears, whispers flutter among the forest creatures, speaking of an ancient stone circle where spirits dance beneath the full moon. Together, we become part of that ethereal landscape. With each shared moment, our bond intensifies, mingling stories, laughter, and a longing transcending words. Soon, we find ourselves in a nearby meadow, alive with blooming wildflowers.

Unity Under the Moonlight - Beneath the moon's benevolent gaze, we find unity in our love, our bodies entwined in a symphony of passion. The air crackles with energy as if Mother Nature rejoices in our union. As dawn's first light breaks across the horizon, we vow to cherish this remarkable night. So, under the summer solstice, Lowena, the forest maiden, and I weave our love story, a witness to the ageless bond between nature and the spirits of the wild.

Scene 9 - Lyonesse

The Haunting Echoes of Lyonesse

As twilight descended, the sky was painted with eccentric shadows, a canvas of darkness unfurling as the last light of day faded. Lowena and I cautiously unearthed a decaying stone edifice, its once splendid exterior now aged and cloaked in creeping vines. The yawning archways whispered of a long-forgotten history.

"This could be it," I murmured, my voice trembling with dread and excitement.

Lowena's wide eyes sparkled with both fascination and fear. "You mean," she asked, glancing nervously at the crumbling stone, "could this be Lyonesse?"

I gestured toward the dilapidated remains, feeling an electric thrill surge through my veins. "The legend tells of a city lost to the sea," I replied, "but could it be here, concealed by the forest?"

A chilling wind whipped through the archways, carrying with it the faint scent of saltwater and decay, thickening the atmosphere with an unsettling dread. Every shadow deepened, contorting like vengeful spirits lurking just beyond our sight. A jolt of apprehension surged through me at the sound of a faint scratching coming from within the ruins.

"Did you hear that?" Lowena whispered, her voice barely above a breath.

I nodded, heart racing. "We should go toward it," I said, surprising myself with my calm tone. "We need to find out what's causing that noise."

As we ventured deeper into the maze-like ruins, the scratching grew louder, echoing through the desolate passageways. Intricate, faded frescoes adorned the walls, depicting long-ago battles and forgotten rites, ghostly reminders of a city long succumbed to time.

"Look at that," Lowena pointed, her eyes wide as she traced her fingers over the chipped remnants of art. "It's like they're alive."

Just then, a blood-curdling scream shattered the oppressive quiet, piercing through my thoughts. Lowena gasped and stumbled back, her face drained of colour. "What was that?" she cried, clutching her chest.

"I don't know," I replied, gripping her hand tightly and pulling her close. "But we shouldn't be here."

As we turned to flee, a shadowy figure emerged from the gloom. My heart raced as I focused on her: a young woman with hair like spun gold stood by a fountain, her eyes filled with haunting sorrow. She reached out a delicate hand, fingers almost otherworldly as if woven from moonlight.

"Don't stay," her voice floated to us, soft yet urgent, echoing through the chamber. "This is a world lost to time. Don't stay; this world is not meant for you."

A freezing chill enveloped me, and I understood. Memories steeped this place, frozen echoes of a vanished world.

"We have to get away," I urged as the salt spray stung our skin. We scrambled over wind-swept rocks, the desolate landscape bearing down on us. Rounding a jagged wall, we stumbled upon a narrow opening concealed by a veil of seaweed and kelp.

"Could this lead to Lyonesse?" I wondered aloud, brushing the seaweed aside.

Lowena squeezed through first, her breath quickening. "It smells ancient in here, doesn't it?" she remarked, wrinkling her nose at the damp air.

The narrow passage opened into a cavernous space, vast and echoing.

Moonlight streamed through a gap in the ceiling, illuminating a breathtaking sight.

"Look!" Lowena gasped. "It's beautiful!"

Before us, sprawled a city suspended in time. Towers of pale stone loomed high, their windows emanating a soft glow, while the streets lined with moss-covered stones awaited the return of their forgotten residents.

As we wandered through the enchanting streets, my footsteps echoed in the stillness. "Do you hear that?" I asked, straining to catch a distant melody that hummed in the air.

"Yes! It's almost like… laughter," Lowena replied, eyes wide as she ran her fingers along the crumbling walls.

But around us, life had long faded, leaving only a haunting void. Once a thriving hub of fishing and mining, the city lay deserted, its structures crumbling and roads silent, weaving a story of reliance on the unyielding march of time.

Lowena reached a dilapidated church, its steeple reaching toward the empty sky. Stepping inside, the hollow reverberation of her footsteps echoed through the sanctuary. "What happened here?" she whispered, staring at the shattered stained glass casting mournful light.

"It's as if they just… vanished," I replied, my voice almost lost in the suffocating atmosphere.

Lowena's gaze drifted, her expression shifting to one of deep sadness. "There's a hollowness here," she muttered, reflecting her own solitude. "It's like—"

"Like something inside is just—missing?" I finished for her, feeling the weight of the desolation that surrounded us.

As darkness deepened, we sought refuge in an abandoned house. Moonlight filtered through the shattered windows, casting ghostly shapes on the walls. The silence was overwhelmingly profound, broken only by the rhythm of our hearts.

"That's it," Lowena murmured, clarity in her eyes. "True desolation isn't just an absence of life. It's a void that lingers in the soul, isn't it?"

"Yes," I agreed, feeling the truth of her words seep into me. "It's the loneliness that consumes us."

We lay beneath the remnants of a life once lived, our thoughts alive with the haunting echoes of Lyonesse. When we retraced our steps, the eerie visions of the city stamped in our memory, we emerged from the passage, breathless and shaken. The moon had vanished, and darkness swallowed everything.

"The opening…" I stammered, looking around. "It's gone!"

"Come," Lowena urged, her tone resolute, "let's find a shelter where we can ease our weary spirits."

She guided me away, and the stillness of the air and the tranquillity of the water offered a sharp contrast to the upheavals we had witnessed. A modest hut, constructed from driftwood and reclaimed materials, sat nestled by the bank, its windows glowing with the warm flicker of a fire inside.

"It's a fisherman's hut," Lowena explained, her voice softening, a glimmer of hope shining in her eyes. "He's gone for the night but left the door open for us. We can find rest here."

Without any more second thoughts, we stepped inside, instantly engulfed by the fragrance of wood smoke and sea air, a much-needed relief. The fire crackled in the hearth, casting playful shadows on the rugged walls and soothing us. We drew close together, our bodies discovering comfort after a long, challenging journey.

The memory of Lyonesse lingered with me, a vivid reminder of life's fleeting essence and the delicacy of existence. Deep down, I sensed the city slumbered below, patiently awaiting the moment it could rise again. We shared a silent understanding, the wind whispering our unvoiced anxieties, binding us to the lost echoes of a world forgotten.

"My Lovely Lady" is a lyrical homage to love that is both tender and grounded in the natural world. It invites you to reflect on your own experiences with love, beauty, and the desire to hold onto moments that feel too brief. The song is not just a love letter to a person but also to the enchanting environment surrounding us and enriching our relationships. In a world that often rushes past, "My Lovely Lady" is a gentle reminder to savour and protect the beauty of our loved ones and our world.

Chapter 4

"Song 4 Narrative - I'll Help You Land"

A State of Well-Being

Life often feels like a complex maze where sadness and depression entwine together like sorrowful strands. For me, sadness is a familiar visitor, an old friend, a momentary presence that arrives in the wake of disappointment. It crashes over me in waves, much like the relentless tide, leaving me soaked in despair. Yet, those waves subside with time, revealing the shore of contentment once more.

My past, however, tells a different tale. Depression enveloped me like a heavy, suffocating blanket, engulfing my thoughts, emotions, and actions and turning me into a living embodiment of melancholy. Unlike sadness, which is triggered by specific events, depression is cruel and relentless. Even in moments of good fortune, it clung to me like a sinister parasite, sapping me of all joy and hope.

My gaze became distant, my expression blank. The vibrant world around me seemed to mock my colourless existence, and my heart ached with sorrow for myself. Yet, I decided to seek a beacon of hope for better days to come.

Reaching out, I found a compassionate listener near me who bestowed her encouraging words and reminded me I was not alone. I shared both my struggles and victories. With time and constant support, I emerged from that overwhelming darkness. The grip of depression loosened, allowing moments of joy and fulfilment to seep back into my soul. I felt what it was like to feel happiness again. While sadness still lingers in my life, it no longer casts a shadow over my existence. My fourth song, "I'll Help You Land," is a tribute to that journey. I found solace and inspiration in the unwavering support of an extraordinary woman, compassionate and wise.

Song 4 – "I'll Help You Land"

I'm a round-about
Circling round
Round and round I go
I've been blessed with happiness
In a sky of fluffy clouds
You're a broken bird; come take my hand
I'll help you land

Stay in my castle; you'll be safe
You'll be safe with me
I'll leave the drawbridge down; you'll feel free
You'll be free always, free
When you're falling, I'll catch you; if I can, I'll help you land

I'll take your part
I'll hold you close to my heart
When you're falling, I'll catch you if I can; I'll help you land

I'm a round-about circling round, round and round I go
I've been blessed with happiness
In a sky of fluffy clouds
You're a broken bird; come take my hand
I'll help you land

Scene 10 – Courage

Standing at the edge of the turbulent river, I felt a wave of fear wash over me. The water rushed downstream, twisting and turning wildly. The crash of water against rocks echoed in our ears, and the mist from the rapid flow kissed my face.

"I came here to escape," I murmured, trying to find calm amidst the chaos. "I wanted to find peace."

Lowena, standing beside me, turned her gaze toward the surging water. "Sometimes, peace isn't about finding a quiet place," she said gently. "It's about confronting what frightens us."

A fleeting sense of regret washed over me as I remembered my purpose for this journey. The allure of this raw, untamed environment had drawn me in, yet it was now intimidating. I took a step closer to the river, my adrenaline surging as I felt the power of nature pulsing in the air.

"Look at the sunlight on the water," Lowena pointed out, her voice filled with awe. "It's almost hypnotic, isn't it? There's beauty in the chaos."

"Yeah, it does have a strange charm," I admitted, resting my hand on the rocks. "Maybe it's not just about running away. Maybe it's about facing fears and embracing the unknown."

Lowena smiled at me. "You don't have to do it alone. I'm right here with you. Remember, courage isn't the absence of fear. It's the determination to move forward in spite of it."

I nodded, sensing the courage that Lowena's presence instilled in me. "Courage is a conscious choice. It's fueled by love and purpose. I think I can do this. It might be tough, but I won't grow if I don't try."

Gathering my strength, I closed my eyes, inhaled deeply, and steadied myself. "The river is our path. Destiny waits for us on the other side."

With newfound determination, I opened my eyes and stepped forward. The cool water engulfed my feet, and the furious current roared around us. I looked at Lowena as she grasped my hand tightly.

"Together!" she called out, her spirit unwavering.

As we pushed forward, the river fought back, trying to sweep us away. "We can't give up now!" I shouted, feeling the torrent tugging at us.

"We'll battle it!" she urged. "Summon all your strength!"

We stumbled and fell, the water splashing around us, but every time we fell, we rose again, fueled by determination. As the sun began to set, casting golden hues over the water, we caught sight of the opposite shore.

"We're almost there!" I exclaimed, pushing myself harder.

Finally, we reached the other side and collapsed on the bank, exhausted but victorious.

"We did it," I breathed, a sense of pride swelling within me.

"Not just in crossing the river," Lowena said softly, "but in learning what it takes to face our challenges. It's about the journey, not just the destination."

I reflected quietly on her words, realising how true they were. My journey didn't end with reaching the shore; it was about facing challenges, discovering myself, and understanding the difference between bravery and courage.

"Bravery is the lack of fear," I mused aloud, recalling our experiences, "while courage is confronting that fear. I'll need both to conquer the obstacles ahead."

"And you will," Lowena reassured me, "as long as you keep moving forward."

We sat in silence for a moment, breathing in the scent of the surrounding trees and stones, letting the experience wash over us. The river may have been turbulent, but I had emerged from it transformed, ready for whatever came next.

Scene 11 - A Feeling Of Happiness

The Unpredictability of Life - Like the river, life is full of unpredictability and transformation. We each have our journeys, trying to find our way. Quick decisions and unexpected turns are necessary. But no matter the path taken, we are all interconnected in the endless flow of existence. Those who seem to glide through life's challenges have mastered navigating its complexities. I often long for that same grace and confidence.

Navigating Life's Crossroads - Life rarely unfolds as expected, just like at a crossroads. Unexpected detours can steer us off course, taking us to places we had never assumed we would end up. I have had my fair share of those moments, feeling lost and unsure of what to do next. I remind myself that there are always alternative routes to reach my destination. Trust is essential for navigating life; trust in the self. Even if we don't know our destination, as long as we keep moving forward, we will eventually find our way.

The Journey Forward - Just as at a junction, we might need to make a few extra turns or a U-turn. Every experience and decision guides us towards where we are meant to be and where we are needed. Life can be chaotic and overwhelming, but embracing its flow reveals the beauty in its intricacies. It reminds us that life is constantly growing, urging us to adapt and progress. Like a dancer, we must trust in our steps as we take them, knowing that each move leads us to our unique destination.

The Intersection of Joy - I stand at a junction, feeling like a traveller in a dreamy world. Fluffy clouds surround wherever I turn, and joy rushes to me. It seems as though I have been granted an infinite spring of happiness, compelling me to smile. The world bursts with colours and the sounds of laughter. With Lowena by my side, I bask in pure bliss, letting go of all worries and fears.

Reflecting on the Journey - Amid the whirling ground, I reflect on the highs and lows, the gains and losses of humanity. The journey isn't always smooth, but at this moment, I am engulfed in happiness. I feel fulfilled and excited about the future. People tend to overlook what they already have as they become preoccupied with acquiring more. I refuse to fall into that trap of relentless pursuit. Instead, I will cherish the small moments of happiness and savour them, ensuring I never take them for granted.

Embracing the Present - As the spinning slows, I experience a sense of peace and contentment. Chaos and constant change remain true, but I understand that I must live in the present to focus on appreciating what I have. By doing so, I will carry along a fountain of happiness within.

Scene 12 - A Bird's Fragile Flight

A Village of Colour and Laughter - In the tranquil village of Restormal, life blossomed in colours of ochre and gold. The rooftops glimmered under the midday sun, casting friendly shadows across the cobbled streets where laughter resonated like music. It was a humble place, untouched by the burdens of the royal court, and it was here that Edward, the stoic prince, found an unexpected refuge.

The Weight of Royal Expectations - Edward had grown weary of the relentless pursuit of power that had overshadowed his youth. His mentors had long groomed him to rule, placing a crown heavy with expectations upon him and clouding his soul with ambition.

Yet in Restormal, he was merely Edward, a weary traveller looking for solace. The villagers welcomed him without questions, their kindness wrapping around him like a warm blanket on a frosty night.

The Prince Beneath the Surface - However, Edward did not fit the traditional mould of a prince. He was cold and cruel, moulded by the punishing world around him. England, fraught with endless wars and political strife, left him as a witness to much bloodshed and hardship. Shaped by a domain where power was paramount, he had mastered the art of being relentless in his existence.

Forging Unexpected Bonds - Though he arrived unannounced and assumed an entirely different identity, it wasn't long before he became a beloved figure in Restormal. He roamed the village daily, forging friendships that transcended titles and rank. He helped mend fences beside the farmer, listened to stories spun by the elderly at the well, and joined children in their games of chase, laughter echoing in the air as they darted under swaying branches. Slowly, his shoulders, which had once borne the weight of a kingdom's grief, began to lighten, and a sense of community filled the empty spaces in his heart.

A Meeting with Empathy - It was during one of these playful afternoons that Edward first encountered Lily. She stood apart from the other children, leaning on a walking staff, her small hands cradling a fragile injured bird, its wing bent at an unnatural angle. Unlike the others, who danced in boundless energy, Lily remained serene, her focused gaze reflecting empathy and a wisdom that belied her years.

"What will you do with him?" Edward asked, kneeling beside her. His voice, though gentle, carried a hint of his innate royal authority.

"I'll help him," Lily replied, soft yet resolute. "He just needs some time and a little kindness."

The Awakening of a Heart - Edward felt an unfamiliar tug at his heart as she tended to the bird. It reminded him of the small joys he had forsaken amid the relentless ambition of his upbringing—an echo of innocence he had buried under layers of ruthlessness. There was a deep resonance between them, something shared that transcended their circumstances. At that moment, he recognized how much he yearned for connection, understanding, and purpose.

Transformation in Friendship - Days turned into weeks, and Edward found himself drawn to Lily, her presence igniting sparks of transformation within him. He spent more afternoons with her, helping build makeshift birdhouses and carving toys from wood. With each moment, he shed remnants of his former self. The walls built high by duty crumbled as he discovered the beauty of vulnerability and the strength in compassion.

Lily's laughter was pure and infectious, rippling through the village. She had a way of bringing together the children and even the adults who had grown weary under the burden of life's trials. Her gentle spirit inspired warmth that spread through the community, igniting conversations and laughter across dinner tables. Once a mere backdrop to his existence, the village transformed into a lively display painted with relationships and shared stories.

The True Essence of Wealth - Edward learned the true essence of wealth through her eyes. It lay not in titles or riches but in the bonds they forged together: the quiet moments spent watching sunsets, shared meals, and celebrating the joy of life. He began to understand his scars, realising that they connected him to every villager who faced adversity, laughed, and cried under the same canopy of stars.

A Bittersweet Farewell - Then came the fateful day when the bird, once fragile beneath Lily's care, took its first flight. It soared into the sky, a symbol of the healing power of love. The villagers gathered, cheering, their voices raised in a symphony of hope. Edward watched alongside Lily, a smile illuminating his face as he recognized his transformation reflected in the bird's ascent.

"Oh, Edward!" Lily exclaimed, clapping her hands in delight. "Look how free he is!"

"Yes," Edward replied, his heart swelling with a joy he had not known in years. "He is free."

Yet, as tears welled in his eyes—not of sorrow but of a bittersweet realization—he recognized that though he had come to Restormal seeking respite, he would soon face the obligations of his title and the kingdom waiting in the distance.

The Weight of Responsibilities - As twilight set in, casting a lavender light over the village, Edward walked along the banks of the flowing river, Lily by his side. The laughter of the villagers echoed in the air behind them while fireflies danced in the cooling night.

"Will you stay here forever?" Lily asked, her voice laced with innocence but a hint of earnestness.

Edward sighed. "I cannot, dear Lily. I have a kingdom to tend to and responsibilities to fulfil. But… this place, these people, I will carry them with me, always."

A Legacy of Kindness - The girl, wisdom beyond her years shining in her eyes, took his hand. "Then you must tell them of this place. Of kindness and laughter, of all the love that exists here."

"I will, but I wish they could experience it themselves," he said, lost in thought.

Lily squeezed his hand, her spirit tangible and warm. "They can if you let the moments of joy shape your reign. Be their prince of kindness, Edward."

With the weight of her words settling in his heart, Edward realised that her kindness had transformed him. In Restormal, he had shed the shell of responsibility and expectation. In its place, he wore armour of compassion and community.

As the stars twinkled above them, casting reflections upon the river, Edward knew the truth. He found not only respite in Restormal, he rediscovered himself.

In the heart of Restormal, Edward, the stoic prince, had been reborn. He found a renewed purpose among the ochre rooftops and laughter-filled streets, not as a ruler of men but as a member of a community woven together by shared experiences and compassion. At that moment, he recognised that, no matter where his path led him, he would always carry a piece of this tranquil village with him along his journey, a reminder of the home he found within the love and laughter of the people he cherished.

"I'll Help You Land" resonates as a gentle reminder of the importance of companionship, especially during tough times. It reflects the beauty of human connection and the power we have to uplift one another. The song ultimately serves not only as a reassurance to the "broken bird" but also highlights the mutual

dependence that often exists in relationships, where both parties find solace and redemption through their bond.

Chapter 5

"Song 5 Narrative – Black and Gold"

The Essence of Cornwall

Under the vast Cornish sky, the rhythmic heartbeat of the Atlantic infuses the ancient land of Cornwall with life. United with a harmonious chorus, a celebration of our pride and belonging. Singing of our beloved home, symbolised by our Black and Gold, emblematic of our mining heritage, and our national flower, the gorse.

The melodies reflect the rugged cliffs that border calm shores, carrying a spirit of togetherness. We are not solitary figures but a steadfast community, forever bound by our love for this granite sanctuary.

As the melody swells to its peak, maidens from Cornwall, adorned in traditional dresses of bright saffron and deep emerald, appear from the crowd like shining flowers. Their presence alone ignites a sense of awe and deep respect.

The accompanying dance highlights their strength and beauty, mirroring the spirit of the Cornish people. Each graceful step and twirl encapsulates our identity: resilient, proud, and unyielding. Their movements blend elegance with strength, illustrating the enduring spirit of Cornwall.

"Black and Gold," my fifth song, serves as a potent embodiment of the unbreakable bond that unites every Cornish heart.

Song 5 – "Black and Gold"

High above the lighthouse
where the gannet's fly
way above the ocean
where the sea meets the sky

Trawler boats are fishing
on seas of blue
our brave boys of Meva
the skipper and his crew

And they're singing
God bless this land

of black and gold
our Cornish maids
both young and old
Trelawny's army
one and all
this granite rock is our home

White rivers of kaolin
flowing through my town
from the Cornish Alps
that are landscaped all around

The dust is settling
like snow upon the ground
brass band of St Austell
with their melodic sound
and they're playing

God bless this land
of black and gold
our Cornish maids
both young and old
Trelawny's army
one and all
this granite rock is our home

Scene 13 – Lowena

Lowena and I stood on the rocky shore, the rhythmic sound of waves crashing against the cliffs filling the air with a soothing melody. The setting sun casts a golden glow over everything, making the moment feel even more magical.

"I can't help but smile as I think of the countless hours I spent here as a child," she said, her voice filled with nostalgia. Her eyes sparkled under the warm light. "The waves crashing, the seagulls soaring overhead. It all feels like a beautiful memory that just wraps around you, doesn't it?"

I nodded, soaking in the ambience around us. "It really does. There's something special about places that hold such precious memories. They almost feel alive."

Lowena looked out at the horizon, a gentle breeze playing with her hair. "This cove holds so many stories — laughter and tears. Do you ever feel that way about places you've been?"

"Absolutely. When I think back, certain spots awaken feelings I thought I'd forgotten. It's like each location has its own heartbeat, full of experiences and connections," I replied, feeling the weight of her words.

She smiled, her gaze shifting to me. "And in this village, I used to feel a deep sense of community. Everyone knew each other and cared for one another. I sometimes find that spirit hard to come by nowadays, so I struggle with the changes."

"I can imagine," I said softly. "But I sense that spirit still exists in some form. It's in the way the villagers greet one another, the laughter shared in the square. You've helped me see that."

Lowena's expression brightened. "You think so? It fills me with hope. I've missed that connection. It feels as if, through our friendship, I've started to find it again."

"Definitely," I replied, taking a moment to absorb the beauty around us truly. "Your stories and warmth have shown me the importance of those bonds. Beauty exists in connection, even if it sometimes feels fleeting."

As the last rays of sunlight dipped below the horizon, a serene quiet enveloped us. The cove seemed to hum with life, capturing the essence of our conversation.

"It's incredible how time feels like it pauses in moments like this," Lowena mused, her voice barely above a whisper. "It allows us to reflect, to hold onto what means the most."

"Exactly," I said, looking at her with a newfound appreciation. "These moments, this place — they'll always be with us. A delicate tapestry of laughter, nostalgia, and hope."

Lowena took a deep breath, her smile radiant against the backdrop of the twilight sky. "Thank you, Gerran. For being part of this. You've rekindled something within me that I thought was lost."

I returned her smile, gratitude swelling inside. "And I will carry this connection with me, always."

We sat together in silence, the gentle sound of waves lapping at the shore echoing the unspoken bond forming between us amid the enchanting beauty of Cornwall.

Scene 14 - Kernow

In the distance, the sound of a band resonated as people joined in song, celebrating God's blessings upon their land, voices harmonising beautifully. They sang of their black and gold homeland and the unity of their community. Individuals came together, bonded by their shared love for this place.

As the melody peaked, Cornish maidens in traditional attire took the spotlight, showcasing a graceful dance that paid homage to their strength and beauty. Their movements, a blend of elegance and power, captured the unyielding spirit of their people.

As the day began turning to evening and stars were ready to twinkle above, the people of Kernow gazed at their land with affection and pride; this was home. A beautiful realm that had welcomed many brave souls, it embodied peace and serenity, where the sea embraced the sky, and the view was breathtaking.

Life at Sea - Amidst the calm, an undercurrent of adventure and labour thrived. Trawler boats dotted the waters, nets brimming with the day's catch. Among them were the daring fishermen from Meva, led by their steadfast skipper and loyal crew.

The wind whipped across the 'Lucy Mariana' decks, its salt-laden breath biting against the men's faces. The waves crashed against the vessel's hull, their thunderous roar a backdrop to the men's powerful, unified singing. They praised their land, their granite rock, their Cornwall.

The youngest among them, young Jordan, squinted at the mist catching the setting sun, transforming it into a fiery orb hovering above the wild sea. Eyes as clear as the ocean held a deep yearning for the home they sang about. Having been at sea for a month, fishing the hazardous waters off France, he longed for the rolling green hills, the salty air mingled with heather's fragrance and the warm embrace of the village pub.

The Power of Song - The age-old song began as a gentle murmur, swelling into a powerful chorus celebrating the fertile soil nurturing golden gorse, a vibrant symbol of encouragement. Its bright blossoms signalled hope, promising life and prosperity.

With passionate voices, they hailed the plentiful harvest the sea bestowed upon them. Each verse of their anthem painted images of hardy fishermen brave enough to face relentless waves, returning with the fruits of their labour.

Their song celebrated their land and the unbreakable spirit of their ancestors. They sang of the courage of those who had bravely defended their home, the rugged coastline standing as an onlooker, to the sacrifices made to protect their way of life.

Jordan felt his throat tighten, his heart pulsing with the rhythm—a song of belonging, pride, and an enduring love for their homeland. They were Cornishmen, born of the granite rock.

Wisdom of Experience - Old Tom, the eldest among the crew, weathered by years of sea and wind, turned to Jordan, his eyes reflecting the vibrant sunset. "They say, lad," he rumbled, his voice rich with wisdom, "our land is forged from the bones of giants. We are their kin, born of this rock, and our voices echo their courage."

Jordan gazed at the rugged cliffs rising steeply from the sea, their jagged edges reminiscent of giant bones, and felt a swell of pride. The song was more than just music; it was a story braiding into their very being, a legacy passed down through generations. They weren't just fishermen but guardians of their land, their voices embodying its strength, beauty, and enduring spirit.

As the sun sank below the horizon, the men's voices softened, the song fading into a hum. A peace enveloped the 'Lucy Mariana,' an overwhelming sense of connection to something greater than themselves. They were on their way home, returning to the land that sang in their veins, the granite rock that was their Cornwall.

Unexpected Beauty of Kernow - In the heart of Kernow, amid its enchanting landscapes, an unexpected beauty emerged through mining. Delicate white rivers of kaolin flowed through the village, creating a scene that masked the story of its creation.

Centuries ago, the Cornish Alps had risen, their majestic peaks shaped by the relentless quest for this precious clay, leaving behind imposing spoil heaps that cast long shadows. From this industrial legacy arose a spellbinding spectacle.

As kaolin was extracted and refined, it meandered through a labyrinth of pipes and channels, transforming into white rivers that cascaded down the heaps, leaving sinuous trails. The stark contrast of white against lush greenery created a surreal and fascinating sight.

Perspectives on Industry - Residents and visitors marvelled at the unlikely beauty birthed from human endeavour. The river had witnessed the ingenuity and resilience of the men who had worked in these once- barren hills.

Some regarded the white rivers as symbols of hope, representing the transformative power of industry. They viewed the heaps as blemishes, artistic expressions of humanity's ability to reshape the world.

Others recognised a different beauty within the kaolin rivers. They acknowledged the environmental toll of mining and saw the rivers as poignant reminders of the delicate balance between nature and industry. The white trails served as reminders of the need to preserve the landscapes altered by human activity.

No matter one's perspective, the allure of Kernow's kaolin rivers was undeniable. They represented the delicate balance between nature and industry, illustrating that beauty can emerge from unexpected circumstances.

Flowing white rivers of kaolin continued through the village, illustrative of the resilience that has shaped the land and its inhabitants.

Kernow's rich resources reflect the hard work of its people, with a fine layer of kaolin dust settling on the ground like freshly fallen snow, signifying their dedication and perseverance. Yet amid all the toil, there remained time for joyfulness.

A Breezy Evening in the Village Square - A soft sea breeze rustled through the leaves of the ancient oak that guarded the village square. Below, the cobblestone square bustled with activity, filled with the aroma of baked pasties and a sense of anticipation in the air. Tonight marked the annual Cornish Brass Band concert, and the entire village was eager to join in the festivities.

The Concert Begins - As the first notes rang out, cheers erupted from the crowd. The band, dressed in traditional navy-blue uniforms, stood tall and prepared. Their instruments shone in the diminishing light, and the lively jig that followed had even the oldest villagers tapping their feet. Soon, the square transformed into a whirl of colour and movement, with children twirling with their parents and elders swaying to the beat.

Music that Tells a Story - The music flowed through the streets, enchanting the villagers' hearts. It narrated stories of their ancestors, the rugged beauty of their homeland, and the unwavering spirit of resilience that characterized their lives.

A Shared Connection - With each note, camaraderie emerged, instilling a collective pride in their heritage and a bond created through shared struggles and triumphs across generations.

From Jigs to Ballads - The music shifted from lively jigs to moving ballads, each song capturing the Cornish spirit. When the stirring strains of a traditional sea shanty filled the square, the men joined in, powerful voices singing of the sea's dangers. The women complemented their voices with soft harmonies, adding a layer of wistfulness to the performance.

Joyful Celebration - Children danced joyfully around the musicians; their laughter echoed through the square. It was a scene of unrestrained celebration, full of life and love, all brought together by the melodies of the Cornish brass band.

The Final Note - The final notes hung in the cool night air, and a gentle stillness settled over the square. The villagers exchanged glances brimming with excitement and understanding, their eyes shining with a shared connection.

Sharing the Spirit of the Evening - As they left the square, their voices echoed with the tunes of the evening. The music of the Cornish brass band transcended mere entertainment; it embodied their spirit, heartbeat, and identity.

The song "Black and Gold" is a tribute to the beauty and resilience of Cornwall, particularly emphasising the region's unique cultural, historical, and geographical aspects. The opening lines evoke a sense of elevation and perspective, highlighting the natural landscapes where the ocean meets the sky and where seafaring life thrives. This connection to the land and sea is further reinforced through vivid imagery of fishermen and their boats, celebrating the local community and its traditions.

The mention of "Trelawny's army" invokes a sense of unity and historical pride, referring to the legendary Cornish rebellion against oppression and the fight for local rights.

Overall, "Black and Gold" is both a celebration and a reflection—an embrace of Cornwall's unique identity shaped by its landscapes, history, and the enduring spirit of its people.

Chapter 6

"Song 6 Narrative – Solomon Browne"

The Penlee Lifeboat Disaster

The Storm - The wind howled ferociously, whipping the sea into a chaotic turmoil of anguish. Rain lashed against the windows of the coastguard station, obscuring the unsafe sight of the roiling waters beyond. Inside, tension thickened the air. A distress call came in right after midnight.

The Distress Call - A fishing vessel was trapped in a severe storm near Mousehole, with a dead radio and only the Coastguard helicopter as their lifeline. The storm proved relentless, forcing the aircraft to struggle to stay in the air, let alone reach the stranded ship. Realising the urgency, the Coastguard called for reinforcements from the nearest lifeboat station in Penlee, a close-knit community. They dialled, but no one answered.

The Call to Action - Time was running perilously low. The vessel was taking on water, her lights flickering alarmingly. Finally, after an eternity, the Coastguard connected with Coxswain Trevelyan, a stoic leader known for his calm resolve and bravery.

"We need you on standby, Trevelyan," said the Coastguard officer, urgency lacing his voice. "The helicopter is struggling. If they cannot reach them, we need you ready."

Trevelyan's voice was deep and steady. "We'll be ready."

The Weight of Responsibility - After hanging up, the weight of responsibility settled heavily upon him. He understood the dangers. The treacherous waters and howling winds could easily turn the lifeboat into a deadly trap. Yet he resolved to act. He was the coxswain, and his duty was clear. He donned his coat and stepped into the storm, the biting wind stinging his face. The station was empty, with only flickering lampposts illuminating the scene. The lifeboat bobbed in the harbour, waiting for its crew.

Assembling the Crew - Trevelyan quickly gathered the volunteer crew. Seven men answered the call, a mix of fear and determination on their faces. One of the crew, his weathered face etched with concern, tried to mask his fear as he comforted his son with a reassuring pat on the shoulder. The son longed to join the rescue, but Trevelyan enforced a strict policy. No two family members could be on the same job, a rule that had protected lives in the past and one he would not break.

As the crew boarded the lifeboat, anticipation charged the air. They could hear the helicopter's engine roaring above the wild sea. With a decisive nod from Trevelyan, the lifeboat surged forward, cutting through the waves and heading straight into the heart of the storm.

Into the Storm - Swallowed by darkness, the wind raged against the lifeboat, waves crashing over them. Inside, the men operated with silent urgency, each knowing their responsibilities as they scanned the horizon for any glimmer of hope.

In the brutal embrace of the storm, the wooden lifeboat, built-in 1960 as a durable Watson-class vessel, navigated the turbulent waves, its crew resolute in the face of overwhelming odds. As they plunged into the ferocious storm, its fury only intensified. Lightning illuminated the chaos, casting a surreal light upon the wild sea.

The Rescue Attempt - Undeterred, the lifeboat's crew steered through the violent waters, their hearts racing with fear and resolve. The vessel creaked with each rise and fall, testing its limits. After several attempts, they finally drew close to the beleaguered vessel. The two boats bobbed in the storm like toys in a child's play; hope arose. Four desperate souls, two men and two women, leapt across the precarious divide, drenched in saltwater and fear.

With relief flooding in, the crew dragged the survivors aboard, their shouts barely piercing the storm's roar. But their joy quickly turned to despair when they realised that two individuals remained trapped.

A Tragic Turn - "There are two left on board," the crew radioed, their voices fading into the howling storm. It was the final communication they ever sent. A haunting silence stretched on, punctuated only by the raging wind. The lifeboat's lights, once a signal of hope, were extinguished. The vessel and the lifeboat had succumbed to the merciless ocean. As dawn broke, the storm began to relent, revealing a shattered sea and a profound emptiness.

A Tribute - I composed song six, "Solomon Browne," in tribute to the extraordinary courage of the Penlee crew, who exemplified true bravery. They were, without a doubt, the bravest of men.

Song 6 – "Solomon Browne"

God's hands he sent us forth to sleep
Blue skies above fade where a misty sea-line meets
Battered and bruised, as dark as coal
The roughest seas sometimes calm our heavy souls

So don't go feeling sorry for the freedom that we lost
Lamorna, I'll always love you, and I'm glad to pay the cost

Forging ahead in the black of night
Weary and tired, but we'll still fight the fight
Our Mousehole Crewe with gritted teeth
A hurricane force and the hellish seas beneath

So don't go feeling sorry for the freedom that we lost
Lamorna, I'll always love you, and I'm glad to pay the cost

Solomon, our time with you was so brief
The candles burn, but we don't want your grief
This Cornish land is glorious
Its beauty is plain to see
The roughest seas can calm us, but only
God can set us free

God's hands he sent us forth to sleep

Scene 15 - A Stormy Night

The lighthouse beacon cast a steady glow against the turbulent Atlantic, a beacon of hope amidst the treacherous waters. Solomon, the seasoned captain of the fishing trawler, stood at the helm, his eyes scanning the horizon. The sea was a familiar companion, a vast expanse that rewarded and challenged him over the years.

As darkness enveloped the vessel, an eerie sound reverberated from the depths. Solomon's heart skipped a beat as he peered over the side. A magnificent creature emerged amidst the churning waves: a mermaid. Her bright green eyes shimmered with intelligence, and her long, flowing tail rippled through the water.

In an instant, time stands still. Solomon was spellbound by the creature's beauty and ghostly presence. He had heard tales of mermaids, creatures of myth and legend, but he had never encountered one in the flesh.

In Zennor, a legend spoke of an enchanting stranger who graced the village church with her enigmatic presence. Her name was Morveren, and she possessed a beauty that rivalled the sparkling seas that caressed the coastline. Clad in glistening silks and adorned with intricate jewellery, she stood apart from the simple villagers. Her voice, as sweet as the songs of the larks, soared through the sacred space, leaving listeners awe-struck.

As Solomon leaned over the edge of his trawler, the waves lapping up against the hull, he felt a mix of trepidation and awe at the sight of Morveren. The mermaid floated gracefully in the water, her emerald eyes sparkling in the faint light of dawn.

"Captain Solomon," she called, her voice melodic, weaving through the air like a gentle breeze. "You've braved many storms, but your heart displays a different kind of courage."

Solomon's heart raced. "Morveren, is it truly you? I never thought to meet the legend that has captured the imagination of my village for so long."

She smiled softly, a hint of sadness in her gaze. "Legends are but glimpses of truth, Solomon. Tell me, what do you seek among the waves?"

"I seek the bounty of the sea. Yet, I long for something more profound," his confession tinged with honesty. "I've always felt a connection to this vast, untamed world, but until now, I never understood its magic."

Morveren swayed slightly in the water, her tail shimmering like a thousand stars. "The ocean is alive, full of secrets and stories. It can offer much to those who listen."

"I want to listen," Solomon replied earnestly. "I want to understand the ocean's heart, its mysteries. I have felt a shift since our last encounter, a calling that draws me to the water."

"Then heed that calling," she advised, gentle yet firm tone. "The sea tests us, but it also teaches us. Trust your instincts; they will guide you through turmoil and triumph alike."

"Is it true, what they say about mermaids? That you have the power to see beyond the horizon?" Solomon's curiosity bubbled forth, eager to capture every ounce of wisdom she could offer.

"Every creature of the sea has its gifts, just as every sailor has his dreams," Morveren answered, her expression thoughtful. "It is in the depths that you will find your answers. But be wary; knowledge carries both light and shadow."

"What do you mean?" he pressed, intrigued.

"To know the ocean's secrets is to invite both beauty and peril," she explained, her gaze piercing. "Are you prepared to face what lies beneath the surface?"

"I've already faced the storm," Solomon declared, drawing strength from the memory of his recent battle with the elements. "I believe I can endure whatever the sea has in store for me."

A flicker of admiration danced in her eyes. "Then embrace your journey, Solomon. Remember, the tides may change, but you are the captain of your own fate."

"Will I see you again?" he asked, a pang of longing echoing in his chest.

Morveren's expression softened. "The depths bind us, yet the currents of life pull us apart. Perhaps our paths will cross again when the moon sings to the stars."

As the first light of dawn began to illuminate the sky, the connection between them felt electric yet ephemeral. Morveren spoke one last time, her voice barely a whisper above the lapping waves. "Never forget the magic you feel in your heart. It will guide you as surely as the stars guide the sailor at night."

With that, she dove gracefully beneath the surface, leaving Solomon alone with the knowledge that would forever change his journey on the sea. He stood there, gazing into the water's depths, feeling an awakening of purpose within him, ready to face whatever lay ahead.

The lighthouse continued to shine, guiding the trawler through the treacherous waters. Solomon could not forget the magical encounter that changed his perspective on the world beneath the waves.

Solomon's bravery was even greater than before. He could sense danger before it happened. Solomon could anticipate the tides and currents of the sea and chart the best course for his crew. He also had a unique understanding of the creatures of the sea, and the crew looked to him for advice and guidance.

The little fishing boat had set out to sea to catch the daily haul. The sky above became dark, an ominous shade of grey. The winds were howling, and the waves were crashing against the boat, threatening to capsize it at any moment.

Solomon and his crew were not afraid. They had faced rough seas before and had always come out victorious. They knew that they could conquer anything with God's hands guiding them.

As they sailed further into the mist, the blue skies above faded and were replaced by a thick blanket of grey. The sea line seemed to disappear, creating an eerie atmosphere.

Solomon and his crew were determined to push on. They knew that their families in the village were counting on them to bring home a good catch; with gritted teeth and fierce determination, they continued.

While the storm continued to rage, the boat endured, battered and bruised, shrouded in darkness as deep as coal. Yet, it is often the roughest seas that soothe a burdened soul, and in those moments, the crew finds peace and comfort in the ocean's boundless embrace.

Despite the hardships, Solomon and his crew never regretted losing the freedom they had lost. They understood that the sea was their true home, and they were destined to navigate its waters, ready to meet any challenges.

Sailing on, Solomon couldn't help but think of his beloved Lamorna. She was the light of his life, his anchor in the stormy seas. He knew that no matter what happened, he would always love her and be grateful to be with her.

The night wore on, and the storm showed no signs of letting up. Solomon and his crew forged ahead, their tired bodies pushing through the darkness. They were weary, but they would never give up.

The crew was a force to be reckoned with, with each member showing unwavering determination and strength. Together, they braved the hurricane-force winds and the hellish seas beneath.

The storm finally passed; the crew let out a sigh of relief. They had made it through another night. Thanks to their unwavering faith and determination.

Scene 16 – Lamorna

The Longing at the Cliffs - Lamorna stood on the rugged cliff, her gaze sweeping across the horizon, yearning for any sign of his return. Days had passed since Solomon embarked on his voyage, and each one had been fraught with anxiety as she awaited his safe homecoming. The violent seas and erratic weather tightened her chest with worry, yet she clung to the hope that he would return to her.

Fading Optimism - As a week slipped by, Lamorna's optimism faded. The sea, once calm, had morphed into a raging force, devouring ships whole and leaving only wreckage in its wake. The very thought of losing Solomon to those treacherous waters was unbearable.

A Glimmer of Hope - Then, on a stormy afternoon, she spotted it, a tiny shape in the distance, barely discernible through the thick fog and tumultuous waves. Her heart soared with joy as she realised it was Solomon's ship making its way back to her.

Rising Fear - But with that joy came a wave of fear. The storm raged on, and the seas were unforgiving, making the journey to shore dangerous.

Her hands trembled as she clutched the note he had left her before setting sail, in which he vowed to return no matter the circumstances.

The Moment of Truth - As she watched the ship navigate the angry waters, growing closer with each passing moment, doubt gnawed at her heart. The thought of losing the love of her life to the sea was almost too much to bear. When the ship finally reached the harbour, Lamorna held her breath, praying fervently for Solomon's safety. The ship docked with a resounding thud, and she sprinted towards it, ignoring the others and the jagged rocks that cut her feet.

Reunion and Relief - At last, she reached the ship, and there was Solomon. Weary and bruised but very much alive. Tears flowed down her cheeks as she enveloped him in her arms, overwhelmed with relief and joy at his return.

Lingering Anxiety - As they made their way home, Lamorna couldn't shake the anxiety that still clung to her. The sight of the wild sea only served as a reminder of the dangers he had faced, a persistent shadow over her heart. That night, as they sat together by the fireplace, Lamorna held Solomon's hand firmly, grateful for his safe return but haunted by the fear of losing him again. She understood that the sea would always loom in their lives, yet she also knew love was more powerful than any storm they might encounter.

Facing the Future Together - As the fire flickered softly, casting warm shadows about the room, Lamorna turned to Solomon, her expression a mixture of concern and resolve.

"Do you ever think about how close it all came?" she asked softly, her fingers intertwining with his. "The wild sea, its unforgiving nature… It terrifies me."

Solomon looked into her eyes, sensing the weight of her fears. "I do," he replied, his voice steady yet gentle. "But I'm here now, and that's what matters. The sea can be wild, but it also brings me home to you."

Lamorna sighed, a mixture of relief and lingering anxiety painted across her face. "I know that, but there's always that thought in the back of my mind. What if… what if you have to venture out again?"

He squeezed her hand tighter. "Every journey has its risks, Lamorna. But I promise always to choose to come back to you. You are my anchor in those tempestuous waters."

Her heart swelled at his words, but a frown creased her brow. "It's just hard sometimes, imagining life without you… or facing those moments again when uncertainty grips me."

"Life is uncertain," Solomon acknowledged, leaning closer to her. "But we're stronger together. Whatever storms come our way, we'll face them side by side. It's you and me against the tides."

Lamorna could feel the reassurance in his words, the truth of their bond resonating deep within her. "I want to believe that," she confessed. "I want to trust that our love can weather anything."

He nodded, determination burning in his gaze. "It will. Love has its own strength and way of guiding us through the darkest nights. Let's promise to hold on to each other, no matter what the future holds."

With a small smile breaking through her worries, she replied, "I promise. We'll navigate this life together, come what may."

As they sat there, hand in hand, the crackling of the fire felt like a soothing melody, a reminder that even amid uncertainty, they could forge their path together.

Scene 17 - Family

Homecoming – Solomon reflected standing at the trawler's bow, a rush of emotions surging within him—a blend of relief, joy, and gratitude. The rugged cliffs of Cornwall, etched against the ever-changing sky, seemed to welcome him back like an old friend after a long absence.

The storm that had tested their mettle had faded, leaving behind a breathtaking landscape bathed in a golden hue. It was a beauty he had longed for during the stormy nights at sea, a reminder that even the fiercest of tempests held the promise of calm.

The Scent of Home - He remembered breathing deeply, inhaling the salty air mixed with the warmth of the setting sun. It filled his nostrils with the scent of home, a place woven into his very being. As the village drew nearer, Solomon couldn't shake the feeling that this return was not just to a physical location but to a part of himself that thrived in the embrace of family and community. Each wave that lapped against the hull seemed to whisper secrets of the sea while his heart echoed with memories of bravery, laughter, and fleeting fear.

Lessons from the Sea - Solomon recounted the journey home, knowing that the seas had taught him valuable lessons—about resilience, about faith, and about the importance of guidance, especially from something greater than himself. With each passing mile, he felt the burdens of the past week lift, replaced by a sense of purpose: that his time on the water was not just a livelihood but a calling deeply connected to the lives around him.

A Warm Welcome - As the trawler docked, he stepped onto the familiar wood of the pier, every creak stirring memories of countless returns. The sight of villagers gathered to greet them filled him with warmth, their smiles radiant against the backdrop of his beloved home. It was a scene that brought back echoes of welcoming songs and laughter, cherished moments that he could hold onto amid the uncertainty of the sea.

A Reunion - Amid the village's vibrant spirit, Solomon had spotted Lamorna, and his heart swelled. Her tears of joy mirrored his own, a testament to the love that anchored him amidst the vastness of the ocean. As they embraced, the world around him faded into the background; all that mattered was this moment of reconnection—a reminder that he was never truly alone despite the storms he faced.

The Family Gathering - The evening unfolded like a soft melody, harmonising voices filled with stories and dreams. At the dinner table, his father's tales of previous voyages intertwined with his sister's eager questions, creating a tapestry of family bonds that reinforced Solomon's sense of belonging. As he watched Lamorna's eyes light up with each story, he realised that these shared experiences were interwoven into the very fabric of their lives, bringing a sense of richness that transcended the challenges they faced at sea.

A Moment of Reflection - After the meal, as darkness embraced the village, Solomon found solace on the porch, wrapped in the tranquillity of the night. The stars sparkled overhead, each a reminder of the vastness of the universe and the smallness of his worries. He understood that while tomorrow would bring new challenges—the call of the sea was unyielding—the love and warmth of home fueled his spirit.

A Promise - In that peaceful stillness, Solomon vowed to remember these moments and carry them within him as he sailed into the unknown. He would treasure the laughter, the tales shared over dinner, and the embrace of those he cherished. In this sanctuary of love, he found his true happiness—a lighthouse guiding him through every storm.

The Comfort of Sleep - He felt a profound sense of peace as sleep began to claim him. The return to the harbour was never merely a physical journey; it was a reaffirmation of his purpose, a reminder that he was rooted in love and community and that no matter where his next voyage took him, he would always have a safe harbour to return to.

The song "Solomon Browne" serves as a tribute not just to those lost, but also to the strength of the community and the inherent beauty of the Cornish landscape, reinforcing that while the roughest seas may challenge, they can also lead to introspection and peace. The refrain about God signifies a search for solace and guidance in the midst of turmoil, making this song a powerful meditation on loss, love, and the complexities of navigating life's storms.

Chapter 7

"Song 7 Narrative – St Micheal's Eyes"

The Creature in the Bay

The Creature in the Bay - The wind howled, sending the grey clouds racing across the sky. This was one of those days that made a person feel small, swallowed by the immense world around them. I stood at the top of Marazion, gazing down at St. Michael's Mount while the cold crept into my bones. Before me, the ocean—a roiling expanse of grey that reflected my inner disorder.

I had come here to write, drawn by the solitude, the rugged beauty of the landscape, and the deep history soaked into the ancient stones, all of which sparked my creativity.

A Glimpse of the Unknown - Perched on a worn stone, I felt the wind tugging at my notebook. My fingers traced the lyrics to a mournful ballad I had begun, lamenting a lost love. But the words felt empty, and the rhythm lacked spark. I struggled to bring life to the ink on the page.

Then I spotted it—a flicker of movement amidst the wild waves, a dark form slicing through the grey. It was too large to be a seal and too swift to be a dolphin. Its movements were graceful, almost otherworldly. I watched as it vanished beneath the waves, leaving a ripple that spread like a ghostly touch across the water's surface.

Inspiration from Fear - My heart raced, pounding against my ribs. My breath hitched in my throat, and a fear slithered up my spine. What was that creature? It was something I had never witnessed before, feeling almost ancient, like an artifact from a bygone era.

The wind seemed to howl even louder, a symphony of unease mingling with my uproar. The grey sky above felt oppressive, pressing down on me like a heavyweight.

The Words Flow - At that moment, the words flowed. Not the mournful ballad I had intended, but verses about the bay, the mackerel skies, and the fishing boats returning. I wrote of the day's darkness and the shimmering lights of Newlyn. When I paused, the wind had quieted, and although the sky remained grey, it felt less muggy; the bay too had calmed. Its surface reflected the softening light.

That creature, whatever it was, had granted me inspiration, a means to articulate the darker currents within me.

A Transformation - As I departed St. Michael's Mount that day, I carried more than just a seventh song titled "St. Michael's Eyes." I felt liberated as if I had broken through the walls of my self-doubt. The creature, the fear it instilled, and the raw emotions it stirred had all captured themselves in my creative process.

The being in the bay would remain a mystery, but its fleeting presence had changed me.

Song 7 – "St Michael's Eyes"

Sunset
an orange glow appears
In St Michael's eyes
Pretty little bird
Turning stones, looking for something
Looking for something
Looking for something

The day dims,
The boats come in
From across the bay
Swordfish dance
Without the night, you will never see the day
Looking for something

Looking for something
Mackerel skies won't fade away

I hear thunder in the distance
I can feel the pouring rain
The Newlyn lights are calling me
As they light up the bay
Looking for something
Looking for something
Mackerel skies won't fade away

Sunset
an orange glow appears
In St Michael's eyes
Pretty little bird
Turning stones, looking for something
Looking for something
Looking for something

Scene 18 - The Sunset Over St Michael's Mount

A Child's Wonder - Have you ever witnessed the magical beauty of a sunset over St Michael's Mount? The orange glow of the setting sun casts a warm light.

It was a peaceful evening. People were busy enjoying the last few hours of daylight. A young girl sat on the edge of a pier, gazing out at the water. She was a curious child, always looking for something new and exciting.

The sun, a swollen orange, dipped below the horizon. The air, still warm from the day's heat, strummed with a gentle hum. A flock of gulls cried, and the soft waves slapped against the shore. On the sand, a little girl, no older than seven, chased after a flock of birds, her laughter echoing in the fading light. Her hands clutched a handful of smooth, grey stones, her tiny fingers running over their cool surfaces.

She wasn't searching for treasures, not in the way most children do. She was searching for something that only she, and perhaps the whispering sea, could understand. Her eyes, bright and inquisitive, scanned the shifting sands, each movement a silent question to the ever-changing landscape.

A lone sandpiper, its plumage speckled brown and grey, landed on a rock near the water's edge. The girl stopped searching and watched as the bird preened its feathers with diligent care. A small smile bloomed on her face—a smile that spoke of a connection with the creature, a silent language understood only between them.

As the day surrendered to dusk, a veil of lavender and indigo draped over the sky. Small fishing boats, their sails billowing like white wings, returned from the open sea, their day's catch glistening in the twilight. The fishermen, tanned and weathered by the sun, hauled their nets, their movements rhythmic and familiar.

Then, the air grew heavy with the scent of salt and the promise of rain. In the distance, the sound of thunder rumbled, a low, guttural growl that echoed across the bay. The boats, sensing the approaching storm, sped toward the safety of the harbour, their sails filling with the wind like anxious birds seeking refuge.

In the fading light, the sea shimmered like a sheet of silver, reflecting the deepening colour of the sky. The small girl seated on a rock watched the spectacle with wide, wondering eyes. Around her, the world seemed to prepare for a grand transformation, a shift from the light of day to the embrace of night.

A flash of silver caught her eye, a flash that seemed to dance with the dying light. It was a school of mackerel, their scales shimmering like a thousand tiny mirrors, their bodies weaving in and out of the water, a living reflection of the sky.

The girl watched as the fish, movements graceful and effortless, swam toward the horizon, leaving a trail of shimmering silver in their wake. In that moment, she had a sense of wonder at the beauty unfolding before her.

Then, the first drops of rain fell. They were gentle at first, like tiny diamonds scattered through the air. The rain grew heavier, a steady, relentless curtain shrouding the bay in a misty veil. The girl, feeling the cool drops on her skin, rose and turned her face towards the town, its lights twinkling like a distant constellation across the bay.

She felt a pull, an instinctual call that resonated deep within her. She had to go there, to the light, to the heart of the town—to the warmth and safety it promised. With a last glance at the retreating sun and the gathering storm, she started walking, her tiny figure silhouetted against the darkening sky, a guiding light of hope in the face of the coming night.

The story of the little girl and the sunset was a story of transformation, of light fading and night rising, of the beauty of the natural world, and the unyielding spirit of a child who, even in the face of darkness, knew that a new dawn would always come.

The Watchers - Lowena and I watched. Our bodies still bore the lingering remainder of our transformation. We peered at the frothy waves crashing against the rugged coastline, our hearts pounding with anticipation.

We had come to this secluded beach, seeking a haven to complete our metamorphosis from these mythical beings. The river water we had ingested earlier had begun its work, but the process was not yet finished. Our bodies shimmered and shifted. Our skin was greenish, our hair like tangled vines, and our fingernails sharp like claws, capable of tearing through tree bark.

The wind howled around us, carrying the scent of brine and seaweed. We stood on the windswept shore of St Michael's Mount, our gaze drawn to the strange and unsettling sight that unfolded before us.

A lone large bird, its plumage silver-grey, flapped among the jagged rocks. Its beady eyes searching for something hidden beneath the stones. The once-bright sky faded, casting a gloomy pall over the scene.

Far out on the bay, a single fishing boat made its way back to shore, its sails billowing in the gathering wind. As darkness cloaked the land, the water turned into a murky expanse, reflecting the last remnants of daylight.

Lowena stood, breathless, her wide eyes fixed on the shoreline. "Did you see that?" she whispered, her voice barely reaching above the tumultuous roar of the waves. "That creature… what is it?"

I shivered, trying to shake the chill that gripped me. "It has to be the Owlman," I replied, my voice trembling. "People say it preys on the lost and broken. This… this isn't just a coincidence."

Lowena's gaze darted back towards the rocks, where the glimmer of something caught the fleeting light of the storm. "But why here? Why now?" She took a step back as a low growl echoed in the distance, and the ground seemed to shudder beneath our feet.

"I don't know," I said, clenching my fists, feeling the sharpness of my own fingernails. "Perhaps it's drawn to us… to what we are becoming." I glanced down at my shimmering skin, each ripple reflecting our transformation. "We should leave, Lowena. We need to find shelter."

"But the lights—" she argued, gesturing toward the distant glow of Newlyn. "If we can reach them, we might be safe. We can't let fear dictate our path."

I felt torn, my instincts screaming to run, yet I knew the allure of the lights was powerful for both of us. "Yes, but what if it follows us? What if it senses that we're not fully transformed yet?"

"The only way to complete this is to reach safety," she insisted, determination set in her gaze. "Together, we can face whatever comes."

I met her eyes, and in that moment, I understood her bravery. "Alright," I conceded, "we move as one. But we stick to the shadows and keep an eye on the skies."

"Agreed," Lowena said, her resolve strengthening. "And when we reach the lights, we stay alert. We won't let anything take us down."

As we started our hurried stride toward the flickering refuge, I could feel the storm closing in, the howl of the wind wrapping around us like a living thing. "We're almost there," I called out, trying to drown out the fear in my heart.

Lowena nodded, her face drawn but fierce. "We'll see dawn after this darkness. We must hold tight to that hope."

With each step we took, I felt the weight of the night pressing down on us, yet Lowena's presence pushed away my dread, just as the lights grew brighter ahead. Together, we would confront whatever shadows lingered in our path—Owlman or not.

Scene 19 - A Monstrous Creature

As the sun dipped beneath the horizon, casting a cerise and gold hue over the water, the little girl edged closer to the edge of the pier. Her heart fluttered with that familiar expectation, a feeling that had lingered since she first learned of the fishermen's tales.

Beside her stood an older figure, a friend of sorts, whose expression mirrored the tension that hung thick in the air.

"It's just like they said," the girl murmured, her wide eyes scanning the water for a glimpse of something unusual.

"Yeah, but this feels… different," the figure replied, a tremor lacing their voice. "There's something about tonight that feels wrong."

The fishermen, their faces weathered with fatigue, began to unload their catch, their movements mechanical as they placed the gleaming creatures in baskets. The girl leaned over the edge, curiosity mixing with dread.

"Look at that one!" she exclaimed, pointing to a creature unlike any she had ever seen. "It's so beautiful and strange."

"Beautiful? It looks… sinister," the figure said, swallowing hard. "Where do you think it came from?"

"From the depths, I suppose," the girl replied, her voice barely above a whisper. "But what do you think it wants?"

"I don't know…" came the hesitant response. "But the fishermen look terrified. They haven't caught anything like this before. And it's not just one—there are so many of them."

As whispers began to spread amongst the men, the air crackled with anxiety. One fisherman, his hands trembling, approached them. "Did you see anything in the water?" he asked, his voice tight with fear.

"Only what you brought back," the girl said, her gaze darting between the fisherman and the eerie catch. "Why? What are you afraid of?"

He hesitated, glancing back at his fellow fishermen, who stood huddled together. "There are things out there, things that have been awakened," he finally said, his forehead glistening with sweat. "Something has changed in the sea… something not human."

"What do you mean?" she pressed, a mix of excitement and dread coursing through her.

"There are stories," he began, his voice dropping to a whisper. "Tales of creatures that were never meant to be seen. They thrive in the dark, in the deep… and they hunger."

The girl felt her heart race, but she remained entranced. "But they can't harm us, can they? We're on land."

"Not if they want to," he replied, shaking his head. "We've crossed into their territory now."

From further down the pier, the ominous growl rumbled, cutting through the conversation like a knife. The fishermen fell silent, their faces etched with dread as they turned to the water, eyes widening at the monstrous silhouette emerging from the depths.

"I need to go," the girl whispered, pulling at the figure beside her. "We can't stay here."

But the figure's feet felt glued to the wooden planks. "What if it's not real?" they said, a blend of fear and curiosity battling within them. "What if it's just a dream?"

The girl locked eyes with them, her voice trembling, "It's very real, and it's coming for us. We have to warn others, we have to—"

Before she could finish, a loud splash echoed, and the creature lunged towards them with terrifying speed.

In that moment, all coherence shattered. The fisherman's voice became a distant murmur as panic surged. "Run!" shouted the fisherman, pushing the girl towards the shore.

As the creature's claws slashed through the water, the last thing she saw was its glowing eyes right before everything turned to chaos.

When she opened her eyes again, the world had shifted. She called for the figure, but all that remained was silence—a crushing void where laughter once existed.

"Where are you?" she cried, her voice lost to the unforgiving sea. "Please, don't leave me!"

But the ocean only answered with the echo of whispered fears and the memories of a night that would haunt them all forever.

Scene 20 - Morgawr

The salty air clung to Lowena's skin, a cold, damp kiss that chilled her to the bone. The mist thick and swirling clung to the cliffs like a shroud, obscuring the jagged outline of the coast. She stood at the edge of the beaten wooden pier, gazing at the restless sea. It churned and whispered, a silent symphony of unease that resonated within her.

"He's out there," her grandmother's raspy voice etched in her mind, the words a chilling refrain that had haunted her since childhood. "The Morgawr. The one who sleeps beneath the waves, waiting to rise," she had always dismissed the stories as mere folklore, the product of overactive imaginations and weathered seaside lives. But lately, the whispers had grown louder, the stories more vivid. The fishermen spoke of strange, unidentifiable objects rising from the depths of a colossal serpent with a trunk-like neck, its body dark as a sea lion's.

A shiver ran down her spine. She knew her grandmother had been a woman of reason. A woman who had seen the world with clear eyes. Why would she speak of such a thing, a creature ripped from the pages of ancient legends, unless it was real?

In the heart of the town, an old woman, Agnes, sat by the fire, her wrinkled face a canvas of experience, etched with the lines of years spent weathering the storms of life. She had lived long enough to witness the ebb and flow of the tides the rise and fall of the moon, and the changing seasons. Familiar with the stories and legends passed down through generations, she knew of a creature that had once been known as the Morgawr, lurking beneath the waves.

She watched, the flickering flames danced and swayed, their light serving as a vulnerable beacon in the face of the encroaching darkness. The rumours, the stories, the unease in the villagers' eyes, all confirmed what she already knew. The Morgawr had awoken. Having broken the age-old slumber, the beast emerged from the depths.

Fear gnawed at Agnes' heart, a familiar ache, but it was not fear for herself. It was fear for the town, the safety of her people, a fear rooted in ancient wisdom, in a knowledge passed down through generations, a knowledge of the creature's hunger, its insatiable appetite.

The storm raged a furious dance of wind and water, the waves crashing against the cliffs, spitting foam and spray across the shore. Lowena stood at the edge of the pier. The salty wind whipped at her face her hair a tangle of wild strands. In the distance, she saw something rise from the depths, a dark, serpentine shape, its head piercing the surface, its trunk-like neck swaying. Her heart hammered against her ribs. It was the Morgawr.

The creature's eyes, glowing in the darkness, met hers across the churning water. They were the eyes of a hunter, cold, sharp, and filled with a primal hunger.

The creature turned its massive head toward the town, its gaze sweeping across the huddled forms of the people. A silent scream, held captive by the storm's roar, filled the air with anticipation.

The Morgawr rose, its enormous body surging out of the water its scales glinting the reflecting light of the moon, its shadow stretching across the village. Fear, ancient and raw, boomed in the heart of every man, woman, and child. They knew, in the depths of their souls, that the beast had risen. And it was coming for them. Morgawr, a legendary sea beast, had returned.

Fear gnawed at the town's hearts as the creature drew closer. Its eyes emitted an eerie red light, it displayed a menacing grin with its jagged teeth. Morgawr opened its jaw, a booming roar filled the air.

"RUN!" someone screamed.

People scattered in terror, scrambling the rocky cliffs that surrounded the bay. But Morgawr was faster. It surged through the water, its massive tail smashing the boats anchored in the harbour.

As chaos reigned, Lowena stepped forward. Her eyes blazed with determination, and her body changed. Green leaves sprouted from her skin, and her hair turned a vibrant emerald. She had transformed into a spriggan, a powerful nature spirit.

With newfound strength, Lowena raised her arms. Vines erupted from the ground, wrapping around the Morgawr's body. Thorns shot out from the vines, piercing the creature's scales.

The Morgawr roared in pain, but Lowena refused to let go. She summoned all her powers, and the vines tightened their grip. Morgawr struggled, but it was no use. Lowena's vines were unyielding.

With a mighty heave, Lowena pulled Morgawr back into the water. The townspeople watched in amazement as the creature disappeared beneath the waves, its roar fading into the distance.

As the last of the vines sank below the surface, Lowena collapsed to the ground, exhausted. The town rushed to her side, their faces filled with gratitude and awe. A spriggan, a creature they had once feared had saved them.

Lowena knew the Morgawr was not gone. It lurked in the depths, waiting for the day when it could return. And when that day comes, Lowena would be ready.

As the echoes of the Morgawr's roar faded into the distant waves, the once-panicked townsfolk began to gather around Lowena, their features a mix of disbelief and admiration.

"Lowena! Is it really you?" exclaimed a woman from the village whose eyes still shimmered with fear. Her voice trembled as she knelt beside the exhausted spriggan.

"Yes, " Lowena replied, her voice strained but firm. "It's me. I... I had to protect you."

"How did you do that?" another villager, asked, still catching his breath from the chaos. "We've heard stories of spriggans, but we never believed..."

"I never wanted to be a part of the legends," Lowena confessed, her emerald hair fluttering softly in the wind. "But the Morgawr is a threat to all of us. I felt it in my bones when it rose from the depths. I had to fight back."

A villager reached out, touching Lowena's shoulder gently. "You saved us. The Morgawr could have destroyed everything."

A murmur of agreement rippled through the crowd, but Lowena shook her head, worry etched on her face. "Yes, but it's not defeated. It has gone back to the deep, but it won't forget this. It will return, stronger and angrier."

"Then we must prepare, we can't let that creature do this to us again. We'll need to build defenses, gather supplies—"

"Defenses?" someone shouted from the back of the crowd, disbelief hanging on their words. "How can we fight something like that?"

Lowena stood up, brushing the dirt from her emerald skin. "We mustn't only think of weapons. I can call upon the spirits of nature. Together, we can find a way to hold it back."

"But how can you do this again?" "What if you…?" searching for the right words. "What if you can't?"

Lowena took a deep breath, her determination flickering behind her fatigue. "I will. If it means protecting you all, I will find the strength. The Morgawr knows that I now stand in its way. I need your trust and your courage, for when the time comes."

The townsfolk exchanged glances, the fear in their eyes beginning to blend with something else—hope.

"We'll stand with you, you're not alone in this fight."

The townsfolk nodded vigorously. "Together, we'll face it. And together, we'll be ready."

As the storm began to wane and the first hints of dawn peeked over the horizon, Lowena looked at the faces of her fellow villagers, their resolve igniting her spirit. "Then we start today. The Morgawr may wait in the depths, but together we will write a new story—a story of survival and strength."

Scene 21 – Owlman

The airstream lashed through the Cornish cliffs, carrying rumours of a legend as old as the granite. Legend of the Owlman, born from fishermen's tales and children's nightmares. From Mawnan Smith emerged a creature of the night, a grotesque mix of man and bird. I had always scoffed at the tales. Until the night I saw it on the rocks at Marazion.

It knew my secret, and it is here again. This time it's searching for me. A flash of red caught my eye, a massive shape against the moonlit cliffs. It was enormous, a bird of night, unlike any I had seen before. Its eyes, like embers, locked onto me with an intelligence that chilled me to the bone. Its claws, twisted and monstrous, resembled the pincers of a blacksmith, each one gleaming with a metallic sheen.

Before I could react, the creature swooped down. Its wings, an embroidery of shadows and moonlight, beat the air with a thunderous roar. I fell to the ground, the beast's claws inches from my face. Fear turned my blood to ice. I knew then the stories were true. This was the Owlman.

Then, a strange thing happened. The Owlman's talons closed around my chest, and a searing pain shot over me. I screamed a deep sound that bounced through the cliffs. The world around me shone. The air grew thick with a sickly-sweet scent. The Owlman, its predatory eyes burning with a strange hunger, watched.

The pain continued, transforming my body. My bones cracked and shifted, my flesh grew rough and scaly. Leaves sprouted from my arms, my legs twisted and thick, and my fingers turned into claws. I grew, a terrifying metamorphosis. I was no longer human, but something far more ancient. I was a spriggan.

The Owlman, its predatory gaze fixed on me, seemed to waver. Its red eyes flicked from my spriggan entity to the moon, and back again. There was a flicker of something akin to distress in its gaze. My spriggan form, driven by a newfound rage and instinct, lunged at the Owlman.

Two creatures, both born of the night both terrifying, clashed in the moonlight. It was a battle of ancient forces, the anger of the spriggan against the ferocity of the Owlman. The cliffs echoed with the sounds of our struggle, the screech of the Owlman, my snarls and growls.

As dawn broke, the Owlman, wounded and exhausted, fled back into the shadows of the cliffs. I was scarred and weary. I stood on the beach, watching it go with a strange feeling of triumph and terror. To the town, I was now a creature of legend, a terrifying dark secret that lurked in the heart of the Cornish night.

The legend of the Owlman continues, but now it was thought of alongside another legend, the spriggan. Both creatures are feared by humans who live along the Cornish coast.

Lowena settled against the rough bark of the oak, her brow furrowed in thought. "Do you think they truly understand us?" she murmured, tracing a finger along the ridges of the tree's bark, seeking comfort in its timelessness.

I glanced at her, seeing the weariness etched into her features. "Some do, I believe. The Elder speaks of our kin, the old stories. She remembers—"

"But do the younger ones listen?" Lowena interrupted, her tone laced with doubt. "They see us as creatures of the forest, as threats lurking just beyond the town's edge."

"They have their fears," I replied softly, still coaxing strength back into my limbs. "We also once feared the unknown. It's natural, isn't it? To protect what we love by fearing what we don't understand?"

She nodded slowly but offered no reassurance in her expression. "I wonder if they would have been so eager to protect us had they seen the Mawagr and the Owlman at their worst. We are not always just defenders; sometimes we must become the monsters to fight them."

A shudder ran through us both at the memories of our recent battle. "Then we remind them of that too," I said. "We are a part of this world's balance. They protect us, and we protect them. It's a circle, even if it's twisted."

Lowena closed her eyes and took a steadying breath, the scent of the forest filling her lungs. "Will they accept us back after… after those shadows are over us?" she asked, a tremor in her voice. "What if they see us as something dark?"

I leaned closer, offering a comforting presence. "The townsfolk know the truth of our hearts—of our sacrifices. In the end, it's our actions that reveal us. Not the forms we take."

Just then, the sounds of celebration drifted through the trees, laughter and music mingling with the crisp morning air. Lowena's eyes flickered towards the sounds, a mix of longing and trepidation in her gaze. "I want to join them, to feel that warmth again. But will we be welcomed?"

I squeezed her hand reassuringly. "One step at a time. Let's share our story, remind them why we stand together. We can bridge that gap, bring understanding where there was once fear."

Lowena's expression softened as she took in my words. "Together then," she said, determination flaring in her tired eyes. "For the town and for us."

"Always together," I affirmed, our fingers entwined. "No matter how dark the shadows grow, we'll stand as guardians—both to the townsfolk and to each other."

And with that, we pushed ourselves from the comfort of the ancient oak, embracing the dawn and the challenges that lay ahead, knowing we would face them united.

My song "St Micheal's Eyes" is a journey that is not just physical; it mirrors a transformative process. The act of "turning stones" to uncover treasures beneath the surface highlights the growth, seeking out hidden truths about ourselves, our relationships, or our place in the world. To conclude, the repetitive search for "something" reveals that growth often lies in the exploration itself rather than in finding definitive answers.

Chapter 8

"Song 8 Narrative – The Beast, He Roars"

The Wind Howled Like a Hungry Beast

Pendeen's Shadows - As I walked along Pendeen, the wind blew sand against the crumbling walls of the abandoned mines. Shadows stretching long in the dying light. In the earth's belly, the broken bones of shattered men lay scattered like forgotten relics. I wrote my eighth song "The Beast He Roars."

The Return of the Miners - The ghost of miners returned, their faces imprinted with hardship, their bodies bruised and scarred, their eyes haunted by the darkness they had escaped. They slipped back through the earth's cracks, drawn by an unseen force, an insatiable longing. Some, their bodies shattered beyond repair, returned as wisps of smoke, whispers in the wind. Others, the ones with hearts of stone, remain trapped, tortured souls tethered to the mine's unforgiving embrace.

The Gathering of the Bal Maidens - It was the hardest rock ever known. The darkness had taken its toll. The Bal maidens gather in the gloom. Their dresses were torn, hair tangled, and hands scarred, but their eyes held a fire, a defiant spark that dared to challenge the darkness. Walking through the mine, their footsteps echoing through the tunnels, a melody in the silence.

A Moment of Recognition - The men watched, their faces hardened, their hearts guarded. The maidens did not flinch. They looked at the men, their broken bones, and shattered souls. They saw not the ghosts they had become, but the men they once were.

"The darkness does not define you. You are men, strong and resilient not broken, wounded. Even wounds can heal. You are not just a heart of stone, you are a soul yearning for light, love, for a chance to heal."

A Stand Together - The miners, each with their wounds and scars, stand together. They did not shatter, even though they were broken. In their quest to break free from the darkness that engulfed them, these men found a reason to fight for their lives and souls. In the maidens, they saw a future, a light that promised redemption.

Song 8 – "The Beast, He Roars"

Broken bones of shattered men
Day after day, again and again
They slip between the open cracks
The ones that die someday come back
They come back

The hardest rock makes the hardest men
Day after day, again and again
The darkness closes in around you
Tight like a fist, it will surround you
Surrounds you

And the beast, he roars,
Ooooooh ohhhh
And the beast, he roars,
Ooooooh ohhhh

Chiseled face a heart of stone
Her hands are scared she stands alone
Torn dress and tangled hair
But she don't care

And the beast, he roars,
Ooooooh ohhhh
And the beast, he roars,
Ooooooh ohhhh

Scene 22 – William Ellery

Descent into Darkness - The air is thick with the smell of damp earth and something else, metallic, and acrid, like blood on iron. The darkness presses in, a living thing. I can feel it on my skin, a cold, clammy hand that creeps around my neck, squeezing, squeezing… I force myself to breathe, the air ragged in my lungs, each inhale a rasping scream. The pickaxe feels heavy, a dead weight in my hand. It is the only thing between me and the darkness, the only thing that keeps the fear at bay.

The Knockers - Knockers are small, just the size of a child's fist, made of dark, glistening rock. Deep in the veins of the earth, where light never reaches and even the bravest miner fears to tread. They knock. Knocking on the walls, the timbers, on the heart of the mine, it is a constant, insistent tapping that drives men mad.

Relentless Rhythm - The rhythm is relentless, a drumming in my head that mirrors the beat of my heart, a fear resonating in the vast emptiness. I can almost feel their presence, a prickling sensation on the back of my neck. I know they are watching, their tiny eyes shining in the dark, their laughter a chilling murmur in the silence.

Shadows at Play - My lamp flickers, casting long, distorted shadows that dance and writhe on the walls. The knockers love the shadows. They play in them; they hide in them; they feast on the fear they inspire. They are like the darkness itself. They manifest the fear that burrows deep within the human soul.

Pressing Weight - The air grows thinner, the darkness thicker. I can feel the weight of the earth pressing down, crushing my lungs, squeezing the air from my body. I want to scream, but I know the darkness will swallow the sound, lost in the silence of the mine.

Illusions of Light - I see it, a glint of something, a spark of light in the corner of my eye. I turn, my heart hammering in my chest the pickaxe trembling in my hand. It's just a stray shard of rock, catching the faint light of my lamp. My breath catches in my throat, my hand goes numb.

Flight and Collapse - The knocking is louder now, more insistent, and a frantic drumming flows in the tunnels. It's getting closer, I can feel it. I turn and run, my legs heavy with fear, my lungs burning. I run until my legs give way and I collapse onto the cold, damp floor, my body wracked with sobs.

Swarming Presence - They are there, I can feel it. They are all around me, their tiny bodies swarming, their eyes glowing like malevolent stars in the endless night. I can hear their laughter, a chilling chorus of whispers that wrap around my soul, squeezing the last vestiges of hope from my being.

Embrace of the Darkness - The darkness embraces me, a cold, suffocating blanket. The last thing I see is a flicker of light, a tiny spark of hope that fades, leaving me alone in the endless, crushing darkness. Consumed by the silence, the only sound is the rhythmic tapping of the knockers, a constant reminder of the terror hidden in the depths of the earth.

Trapped in Time - I cannot remember how long I have been down here. Days? Weeks? Years? Time has no meaning in this place. I am just a hollow shell, a puppet controlled by the darkness, my life a flickering candle that burns ever closer to its end.

The Game of Shadows - I am not sure why they have not taken me or why they have not dragged me into the abyss. Maybe they are playing with me, toying with my sanity, feeding on my fear. Perhaps they are waiting for when I succumb to the darkness when my spirit breaks and I become one with the darkness, the mine, with the knockers.

Bound to the Depths - The knocking is relentless, a constant drumbeat that surges in my mind. It is a part of me now, a dark melody that breathes in my soul, a constant reminder of the fear that eats me. It is the knockers' song, and I am their captive audience, trapped in the endless cycle of fear and darkness, forever bound to the depths of the earth, forever haunted by the knockers.

Scene 23 - The Knockers

I remember the day I was born. A tremor shook the shaft, a ripple of energy coursed through the tunnels, and my tiny body emerged from a crevice, slick and grey, a new life taking root in the heart of the earth. My brethren, my kin, greeted me with a chorus of clicks and clacks, their tiny voices echoing through the black emptiness. We are a community, bound by the earth, the darkness, by the shared fear we install in the hearts of men.

Appearance - Knockers are diminutive and ethereal, standing less than six inches tall. Their skin is a deep slate grey, reminiscent of the rich ore that permeates their home. The surface glistens in the sparse light of the mine, almost metallic in its sheen. They are playful, with oversized ears that twitch at every sound and a tuft of wispy, dark hair that seems to float and shimmer, mimicking the shadows around them. Their eyes are striking—small, round, and as black as polished obsidian, catching the light with a mischievous glint that speaks of hidden knowledge and playful antics.

Abilities - They possess the ability to manipulate shadows, bending light to create illusions that can hide or reveal things as needed—often using these tricks to play deadly pranks on the miners. They can also whisper secrets of the mine to those they trust, enabling them to find luck in their endeavors. In times of peril, they can harness the energies of the mine to create barriers or illusions.

The miners are our food, not in the literal sense but in the sustenance they provide. Their terror, their desperation, their screams - these are the things that feed our spirits, that keep us strong and vibrant in the darkness. We torment them with whispers in the dead of night, with phantom footsteps echoing in the silence, with the chilling sensation of something small and unseen brushing against their skin. We are the unseen hand, the cold breath, the whispering shadow that haunts their every move.

The new miner arrived a few weeks ago. They called him William Ellery, a young man with eyes filled with a foolish spark of hope. He was new to the darkness, the whispers, to the fear. We watched him from the shadows, marvelling at his naivety. He believed the tales of the knockers were mere superstition, a way to keep the men in line. Silly boy.

We played with him, at first muttering his name in the darkness sending chills down his spine with our tiny cold fingers. He would jump, startled, his eyes wide with fear, but he would always brush it off, attributing it to his imagination. He was the first miner to laugh at us, to dismiss our power. It was a challenge, and we accepted it.

The game went on for days. William, though increasingly nervous, remained unconvinced. Then, one night, we decided to escalate. The air in the shaft grew heavy, the silence oppressive. As William worked, his pickaxe striking against the rock, a coldness seeped through his boots.

He stopped, feeling a prickling sensation on his skin. He looked around, his eyes wide with fear, but saw nothing. He brushed it off as a trick of the mind.

Then we struck.

The tremor reverberated through the shaft, jolting William as he gripped his pickaxe. "What was that?" he muttered to himself, scanning the dim surroundings. Shadows danced, stretching and contracting, but he dismissed them with a shake of his head. "Just my imagination," he reassured himself, though a bead of sweat trickled down his brow.

A faint clicking sound echoed from the depths of the tunnel, causing him to shiver. "Is someone there?" he called out, trying to mask his unease with bravado. Silence responded, wrapping around him like a heavy cloak. He chuckled nervously, brushing off the chill that settled in the pit of his stomach. "It's just stories the old crows tell to scare the newbies."

Hours passed. As William worked, the air grew heavy. He paused, the prickling sensation crawling up his arms. "Come on, don't be ridiculous," he scolded himself. "You're just being a baby." But he couldn't shake the feeling that he was being watched.

The whispers began, soft and teasing. "William…" a voice slithered through the darkness. "William…"

"Who's there?" he called out, panic edging into his voice. "Show yourself!" The echoes of his own words taunted him, a chilling reminder of his solitude.

The clicking sound intensified, morphing into a chaotic symphony of skittering movements. William's heart raced as he felt a rush of cold wind sweep over him, chilling him to the bone. "It's just the wind," he tried to convince himself, but doubt gnawed at him.

The echoes grew louder. "Foolish boy…" they seemed to chant, a chorus of tiny voices resonating from the shadows.

"Stop it! This isn't funny anymore!" he shouted, fear overtaking his bravado. He dropped his pickaxe as the sound of their laughter—tiny, cold, and mocking—filled the air.

With his heart pounding, William stumbled back, hitting his head against a jagged rock. The sharp pain took the breath from his lungs. He lay still, gasping as the darkness flooded his vision, drowning out the sound of his breath.

As the silence settled again, a small voice emerged from the shadows. "Another one lost to the dark. What a sweet feast of fear he has left for us…"

"And soon, his fellows will come," another chimed in. "They will bring their trembling hearts and trembling hands. We shall feast again!"

"Let them feel our power," came a soft whisper echoing through the tunnel. "We are the shadows that haunt their dreams. We are the knockers, and they are but fleeting moments in the dark."

A silent agreement rippled among the spirits. "Yes, always watching, always waiting… They cannot escape us."

And with that, they retreated into the shadows, knowing that the cycle of fear would soon begin anew.

Scene 24 - The Tunnel Collapses

In the rugged expanse of Kernow, deep in the heart of the countryside, lay the bustling tin mines that fuel the industry.

For centuries, men have toiled in the dark dangerous tunnels, extracting the valuable ore that has brought wealth to this land, but as the demand for tin grows, the mines need more workers, and that is when the tough Bal Maidens of Kernow step in.

They are the wives and daughters of the miners, strong women who have grown up in the shadow of the mines. They know the dangers and hardships of working in the mines and are not frightened to get their hands dirty. With their husbands and sons working long hours in the depths of the earth, these women take on the responsibility of managing the household and providing for their families.

With her strong work ethic and determination, Charlotte proves she is as capable as the men in the mines. She has learned to operate heavy machinery, to handle the explosives, and to navigate the treacherous tunnels. She works side by side with the men, her skirt tucked into her trousers and her hair hidden under a cap, never letting her femininity hold her back.

Charlotte is a strong-willed lady, born and raised in the tin mines of Kernow. She is no stranger to hard work, having grown up in a family of miners. Her father had taught her the ins and outs of the industry, and she had learned the trade.

Her life was forever changed when her father, John, died in a mine failure. It was a tragic accident that could have been prevented if the mine owner had provided better safety measures. His loss devastated Charlotte, but she refused to let it defeat her.

Levant mine is in the small town of Pendeen. Here is where the miners work for hours, digging deep into the earth in search of tin. The mine is one of the oldest in the area, with a rich history, but it is a bleak world, where broken bones of shattered men are scattered among its remains. Day after day, men slip between the open earthy cracks, trying to avoid the dangers that lurk in the shadows.

Hard at work, they hear a loud knocking and rumbling coming from deep within the mine. The walls shook and the ground trembled beneath their feet. A disaster is about to strike.

I appear from the shadows. I can see the miners' fear. They had never seen a spriggan before, but they had heard stories of our courage and knew I was their only hope. The men had just completed their shift and headed back up to the surface when they felt the loud rumbling sound. They stop in their tracks, hearts racing. Quickly, they make their way back to the main shaft. Here they find the other men in a state of panic.

The tunnel collapses as they try to make sense of the chaos around them. Men shout, their voices trembling with fear. 'We need to get out of here, now!' Hearts sink as they realise the severity of the situation.

They are trapped.

As we step into the chamber, the oppressive energy surrounding us grows heavier. I take a moment to assess the situation, feeling the air thrum with tension. The miners around me shift uneasily, their eyes wide with fear and wonder.

One miner, his voice shaking, speaks up. "What is that thing? Is it… one of the knockers?"

I nod slowly, feeling the weight of his words. "Yes, it appears to be their true form. This is what has haunted these tunnels for ages."

Another miner, braver but still cautious, takes a step forward. "Can we banish it like we did the others? We have the power, don't we?"

The colossal entity lets out a deep, rumbling laugh that seems to echo off the walls. "You think you can control me, little mortals? I am the essence of chaos in this darkness! Your banishment means nothing to me."

A third miner whispers, his eyes flicking nervously between the entity and me. "What if it's right? What if we're out of our league?"

I take a deep breath, squaring my shoulders. "We are not alone. Together, we can confront this creature. It feeds on our fear; we must stand firm."

The entity leans closer, its glowing eyes boring into mine. "Courage is admirable but also foolish. You believe your strength can overcome centuries of power?"

I raise my voice, unwavering. "We have faced the chaos you've unleashed. We've sealed away your kin. It ends here, today."

The miners rally behind me, their expressions shifting from fear to determination. "We are here to reclaim our home!" one shouts, emboldening those around him.

The entity sneers, "You think mere mortals can reclaim anything from me? I am the shadows that haunt your dreams, the wickedness that lurks in your hearts."

I gesture for the miners to form a circle, planting our feet firmly. "If we combine our wills, we can force it back. Together!"

"Together!" echoes the group as they gather closer, their previous fear morphing into a united front.

The entity's expression darkens, the flames in its eyes flickering. "Foolish spirits! You will regret this decision."

With our combined energy, I channel the power of the earth, feeling its roots intertwine with our resolve. "We will show you what we are made of!"

As we lift our arms, the light within the chamber intensifies, illuminating the strange symbols engulfing the walls. The radiant energy begins to push back against the entity as it struggles, its cruel grin faltering.

"NO!" it bellows, its voice shaking with rage. "You cannot harness what you do not understand!"

But I smile, a newfound confidence surging through me. "We understand more than you realize. We refuse to let fear govern our lives any longer!"

The light expands. The miners around me join hands, reinforcing our bond, and the air crackles with power as we unleash our energy in a united wave. The entity shrieks and contorts, the shadows wrapping around it starting to fracture.

"Retreat!" the entity demands, panic creeping into its voice. "You cannot do this!"

"No," I declare, my heart pounding with determination. "We can. And we will."

With a final surge, we push the entity deeper into the shadows, where its form begins to fade. As the chamber fills with light, we feel the oppressive weight lift, echoing through the tunnels with a newfound clarity.

"Together," I whisper to the group, "we've reclaimed our home."

And as the last remnants of darkness dissolve into the air, we know the knockers have been sealed for good, at least for now, and together we have a future filled with light and courage.

Scene 25 - A Heart of Stone

The news of the commotion beneath the surface spreads like wildfire, and soon, the whole town gathers outside the mine, waiting for any updates. The families of the trapped men and maidens are in a state of despair, praying for their loved ones' safe return, and amid it all, the mine, like a beast, roars. Its howls echo through the empty shafts, a warning to those who dare to challenge its rule.

There is one figure who stands out in the chaos. Charlotte had a chiselled face and a heart of stone. Countless battles with the hard stone have scarred her hands, and she stands alone, a warrior in her own right. Even though her dress is torn and her hair is tangled, she doesn't care. Despite enduring for such a long time in this world, nothing can shatter her spirit as the beast roars once again. With a voice filled with defiance, she sings along with the beast.

In this broken world, it takes a heart of stone to survive, she is the embodiment of that strength, a symbol of hope for those who still cling to the hope of a better tomorrow.

After an eternity, Charlotte and a rescue team reached the trapped miners. The cheers and cries of relief spread throughout the town as the rescue team brought the miners back to the surface, one by one.

Fifty miners had been working in the tunnel, and fifty were successfully rescued. As we emerge from the tunnels, the townspeople cheer.

Abandoned, the mine, once thriving, now rests as a tomb of rusted machinery and forgotten dreams. The knockers were sealed in the deepest tunnel, their cries forever swallowed by the earth. Restless are the knockers, their souls forever trapped within the stone, constantly seeking an escape.

Deep in the heart of the mine, William's spirit is released. The air is filled with the metallic tang of iron and dust.

The spirit descends into the labyrinth of tunnels, a shiver of unease watched and followed by unseen eyes in the darkness.

A rhythmic clicking starts, faint at first, then growing louder. It's a series of sharp, metallic noises, like a hammer against a stone.

The clicking stops abruptly. Silence reigns, heavy and suffocating. The spirit moves forward looking for any sign of movement, anything that might explain the strange sounds.

The clicking resumes, this time closer, coming from the tunnel ahead. It is a rhythmic pattern, like a code, a series of taps and clicks in a specific sequence. The spirit recognises a pattern of the ancient mining code, a signal used to communicate in the darkness.

A wave of icy dread. The knockers using this code, their desperate pleas for release, their tortured souls yearning for escape.

The clicking turns into a pounding, a frantic rhythm that reverberates through the very earth.

The spirit of William sees them.

In the depths of the tunnel, where the flickering light struggles to reach, there are figures, hunched and shadowy. Their eyes, hollow and black, fix upon you. Their skin is a pale, grey, their limbs gaunt and twisted. And they are wearing clothes of miners, their faces obscured by grime and dust.

They move, their bodies swaying like puppets on invisible strings, their movements jerky and unnatural. They raise their hands, their fingers contorted and strike the walls, their fists banging to the clicking rhythm.

A cacophony of raspy whispers and desperate pleas emanated from the knocker's voices. In the tunnels, there is an intensifying clicking, a relentless chorus of despair.

The ground trembles. There is a rumbling, a deep, guttural moan that seems to shake the very foundations of the mine.

The knockers are rising, their bodies contorted, their limbs clawing at the walls, their faces etched with a hunger that transcends the mortal world.

The clicking, the whispering, the rumbling – they all become a single, horrifying symphony, an instrument to the unspeakable terror that lies hidden beneath the earth.

The chilling clicks and clacks will forever echo, a constant reminder of the horrors that await in the depths, the knockers waiting, sealed in their tomb, their souls forever trapped, seeking release.

In essence, the song invites listeners to reflect on their own struggles with the "beast" within—recognising that while the roar may seem terrifying, it can also signal a profound awakening to one's true strength. The protagonist's journey is more than mere survival; it is a reclamation of self, suggesting that through the acknowledgment of pain and the embrace of inner strength, true transformation can flourish.

Chapter 9

"Song 09 Narrative – Nothing Changes"

The Game of Life, Change, Truth, and Resilience

The Craving for Connection - The ninth song, "Nothing Changes," was a political song I wrote. In a world that often seems unrestrained and uncertain, we crave genuine connections, those fleeting interactions that deepen our understanding of our shared lives. The phrase "Come on in and close the door" conveys a feeling of intimate closeness, inviting someone to open up themselves, their thoughts, experiences, and perhaps even the untold secrets they have hidden away from most of the world. It beckons us to pause, enjoy a warm drink, and savour the brief joy of human connection.

The Illusion of Change - As we navigate the complexities of life, from one maze to another, one catchphrase rings true, "It's still the same, nothing's changed, it's just a game." This sentiment underlines a fundamental reality of the human experience. Despite the countless challenges and changes we encounter, an uncanny constancy persists. It hints at the recurring nature of existence, where we grapple with familiar concerns, fears, and aspirations. History has a way of repeating itself, often tangling us in cycles that make progress feel elusive.

The Frustration of Being Unheard - In our information-saturated society, we find ourselves feeling unheard. "No one listens to a word we say" captures the frustration of being overshadowed by the discord of competing voices. It speaks to the existential dilemma of seeking truth amidst a barrage of misinformation, half-truths, and altered stories. A declaration that "there is no such thing as truth" is often shaped by individual perspectives, perceptions, and cultural contexts that bathe in a transparency that has a way of shining light all around and liberating everything around it, as the nature of truth is.

Finding Peace in Simplicity - Amidst these overwhelming intricacies, we discover peace in simplicity. "Take your time and count to five. Thank your God that we're still alive." This message encourages us to slow down and cherish the small moments, the little things that signify our survival, resilience, and the true essence of life. In a landscape filled with uncertainties, reflecting on our existence stirs the fog in our minds away and raises clarity and gratitude for what we tend to overlook in our attempt to pursue the heart's desire. Rather than getting swept away in the chaos, we can draw strength from shared experiences of vulnerability and honesty.

The Call for Self-Care and Healing - We reflect inward, and we inevitably face parts of ourselves that may feel fractured or incomplete. "Take your broken soul from off the floor" is a powerful rallying cry for self-care and healing. While life's struggles may leave us scarred and bruised, they also pave the way for renewal and resurgence. The essence of resilience lies in our capacity to learn from our experiences, reassemble our fragmented selves, and emerge rejuvenated.

Embracing Life's Contradictions - Recognising the repeated nature of our struggles also brings attention to the essential contradictions life presents. The phrase "it's just a game" suggests that sometimes our challenges can feel trivial in the grand scope of life, yet their emotional significance is deeply personal and heavily weighted. By viewing life as a game, we can uncover the playfulness we might overlook, the laughter amidst tears, and unravel the connections we share with others on this journey.

The Power of Conversations - The conversations we engage in, whether over coffee with a friend or during quiet contemplation, shape our understanding of life's intricacies. They help us navigate the challenges of change, the maze of truth, and the unavoidable game we participate in.

Enriching Our Ongoing Story - As we collect our thoughts, we find a sense of shared humanity in our struggles and victories, reminding us that while it may seem like nothing changes, every experience enriches our ongoing story. We live, learn, and through it all, we remain active participants in this complex game called life.

Song 9 – "Nothing Changes"

Come on in and close the door
Tell me something that I've never heard before
Have a coffee, take a rest
Don't you know, my friend, we've been heaven-blessed

It's still the same
Nothing's changed
It's just a game

It doesn't matter anyway
'Cause no one listens to a word we say
Take the lies that suit
Don't you know there is no such thing as truth

It's still the same
Nothing's changed
It's just a game

Take your time and count to five
Thank your God that we're still alive
It's still the same
Nothing's changes
It's just a game

It's time to go now, that's for sure
Take your broken soul from off the floor
Take your time and count to five
Thank your God that we're still alive

It's still the same
Nothing's changed
It's just a game

It's still the same
Nothing's changed
It's just a game

Scene 26 – Sarah and Julia

Tucked between rolling hills and verdant valleys, the stunning white peaks of china clay stood as memories of a laborious past that intertwined with legends of memorable moments and tedious days for the local community. Men, women, and children tirelessly worked the mines with their rough, calloused hands, forging a deep connection with the land and with one another. Yet, beneath the layers of dust and toil, a growing discontent simmered, threatening to disrupt the lives of these small, disparate miners.

At the village's heart, where aspirations clashed with harsh realities, stood The Bugle Inn, a humble tavern on a forgotten corner. It had witnessed countless conversations, much like steam rising from the rich, dark coffee brewing behind the bar to personal moments shared under sunsets filling the sky up with colours. Its walls were a patchwork of stories, some spoken by patrons, others etched over time.

As the sun set, casting elongated shadows across the weathered wooden floor, a weary suffragette stepped into the bar. Julia Varley entered, her face marked by sleepless nights and the weight of a heavy conscience, shutting the door behind her with a purposeful thud.

"Tell me something I haven't heard," she said, sinking into a chair and surrendering to exhaustion's familiar embrace. Behind the bar, a spirited woman named Sarah slid a steaming mug of coffee towards her.

"Life's a stage," Sarah teased with a glimmer in her eyes, "and we're all just characters in the same worn-out script."

Julia managed a soft chuckle, a rare sound often swallowed by the tumult of political discussions. "I know exactly what you mean. It feels like the more things change, the more they stay the same. Those in power just continue to make decisions behind closed doors, drowning out our voices with empty promises and deceit."

"Have a coffee," Sarah's suggestion was accompanied by a hopeful note in her voice. "You've got this incredible passion, but it seems to leave you feeling more frustrated than fulfilled."

As Julia took a sip, a momentary comfort washed over her as her gaze was fixated on the bustling world outside the window—a world alive despite her own feelings of stagnation. "It's the same story over and over," she sighed. "Politics feels like a game. We shout, and we clash, but in the end, no one listens to the woes of the honest."

Sarah nodded, resting her elbows on the counter. "Take the lies that work for you," she said knowingly. "But remember, those who steer the tale also shape the reality for all of us."

"That's the bittersweet truth, isn't it?" Julia replied, her brow furrowed with contemplation. "Yet in this game, truth feels like a mirage, always just out of reach."

At that moment, a group of young miners burst into the bar, their exuberant voices creating an infectious atmosphere. They brimmed with passion, embodying the zeal of a generation hungry for change. Julia watched them with a blend of admiration and nostalgia as they exchanged ideas, solutions, and dreams that felt vibrant and alive.

"Look at them," she murmured. "So fiery and full of hope. It makes me feel ancient."

"Experience, my friend," Sarah countered gently, "is the weight of dreams deferred. But it doesn't mean your journey has reached its conclusion. What have you done recently to channel that passion?"

"I'm not certain," Julia admitted, her gaze drifting to the ticking clock. "I've tried, I've fought, yet every time feels like I'm running into a wall of indifference."

"Take a moment," Sarah suggested, her tone warm and reassuring. "Count to five. Be thankful for what you have. Every moment is an opportunity—a new battle to be fought."

Julia stared into her cup, bitterness and hope swirling within. "It's exhausting. Every campaign feels like a repeat of the same old play. I care, but does it even matter if change is all but a myth?"

Leaning closer, Sarah's eyes sparkled with intensity. "It matters to those who are willing to listen. Sometimes, even the smallest voices create ripples that change the tide. You have the power to inspire. Change might not have happened yet, but it always has the potential to come about when least expected."

The bar transformed into a sanctuary, a cocoon where dreams confronted harsh realities. A flicker of hope ignited within Julia, illuminating the darkness she had been accustomed to for far too long.

As the bell above the door chimed, signalling the spirited young dreamers' departure, Julia rose, fueled by a renewed sense of purpose.

"It's time to move forward," she declared, determination etching her features. "I'll pick up my broken spirit from the floor if

I have to, but I'll fight again, even if it seems like nothing will ever change."

With one last gaze at the comforting glow of the bar and at Sarah, who had offered her more than just a warm drink, Julia stepped back into the chaotic world outside—a world ripe for change and brimming with possibilities that she was now ready to seize.

At dawn, the men assembled at the entrance of the Carne Stents pit in Trewoon, the thick air looming with anticipation. Their voices hovered just above whispers as they exchanged the latest updates from the other pits. For weeks, they had been confiding in one another, sharing their stories of meagre wages and the cruel inequities they faced. A hard day's labour often yielded nothing close to a fair week's pay.

Among them was Joseph, a sturdy figure with strands of grey weaving through his dark hair. He stood with clenched fists, weighed down by the responsibilities resting on his shoulders. As the natural spokesperson for the miners, he rose above the quiet murmurings and proclaimed with fervour, "Five shillings! We toil for our families, and we deserve that raise! It's time we demand payments every two weeks, not just once a month! We must band together, unify our voices, and take what is rightfully ours!"

Nods of agreement and applause accompanied by raised fists rippled through the gathering, a wave of solidarity building among the men. A few paces away, Betsy, Joseph's wife, watched with tears streaking her cheeks. She recognised the peril in their fight.

Their family's scant savings hovered precariously between hope and despair. Yet she was all too familiar with the heavy burden of their weekly struggles and the constant vigilance required to make their dwindling resources last.

Scene 27 - Together We Stand

In the glow of candlelight at the Bugle Inn, Julia stood at the front, her voice steady as she addressed the crowd, a sea of determined faces illuminated by flickering flames. The air was thick with anticipation and anxiety about the life that lay ahead for the people.

"Today, we rise not just for ourselves, but for our children, our families, our homeland," she proclaimed. "This is about more than clay; it's about our right to be heard!"

Joseph, standing close by, nodded. "They may think they can silence us, but together, we are stronger! Remember the stories our fathers told us about standing up to oppression? We carry that legacy!"

A man in the back shouted, "But what if they come at us with force? What if they try to break us?"

Julia raised her hand, silencing the murmurs. "We must stand firm! Fear is their weapon, but unity is ours. If we visually and vocally resist, we become an unstoppable force that shall prove to be their reckoning!"

Maria, clutching Carwyn's hand, looked into his eyes. "Do you think we really can make a difference? What if they send in the police again? What if they hurt us?"

"I won't let them," Carwyn replied fiercely, "They might try to crush us under their boots, but we're standing on our own ground. We are fighting for what is true and our right, and that's worth any risk!"

The crowd began to buzz with enthusiasm, voices intertwining in a chorus of agreement. "Together!" someone shouted. "Together!" echoed back from all sides.

Amid this surge of spirit, an elder in the corner, Mr. Phelps, raised his voice, slightly trembling from age yet firm in conviction. "I've seen too many of my brothers fall into despair because they believed no one would stand. But you, you young ones, you have the fire! Don't let it dim."

Julia nodded, inspired by the elders' wisdom. "Yes, Mr. Phelps! We carry all those stories of struggle within us. Our fight is not just for today—it's for every person who came before us and every child who will follow!"

As the meeting continued, voices rose and fell like the tide, weaving a tapestry of shared hope and determination. Each recounted story was a mingling of laughter and sorrow, history uniting with the present as they prepared to march forward.

At that moment, Joseph clasped his hands, drawing everyone's attention. "At dawn, we'll gather again. We'll march into town together. Let them see our strength; let them feel the weight of our united voices!"

"Let them come!" someone yelled out defiantly.

The atmosphere in the tavern shifted a palpable transformation from fear to fierce resolve. The miners were ready to fight not just for the clay beneath their feet but for the dignity and future of their community.

"Tomorrow, we'll show them the strength of unity!" Julia declared, a flicker of triumph in her eyes as countless voices joined in agreement, flooding the tavern with an overwhelming sense of purpose.

As the candles flickered, casting shadows that danced on the walls, the air resonated with their collective strength. Each miner, mother, father, sister, and brother stood as a testament to resilience, ready to face the looming turmoil that awaited them, their voices carrying the weight of resilience forged in the heart of Cornwall.

Scene 28 - A Tale of Unity and Respect

The Enchantment of Cornwall - Cornwall, a land painted with the fierce colours of the Atlantic and cloaked in a rich tapestry of history, is where the veil between reality and legend grows thin. Its cliffs, ancient stone circles, and the haunting beauty of its untouched lands characterise this region.

The Clay Villages - Within this enchanting landscape exist the clay villages, where the underground world boasts deposits of clay that have long attracted potters and artists from across the globe to acquire premium materials to enhance their artistry. Yet, beneath this façade of prosperity lurked a darker reality, a story of struggle, hope, and the ghosts of the past coming to life.

Tension Among the Miners - As summer tiptoed into Cornwall, the miners working in the clay mines wrestled with a growing sense of unease. The life they led was fraught with hardship. Their plight engulfed by the damp, dark tunnels beneath the earth, battered by poor wages and oppressive working conditions that looked to grow worse with each passing day.

Unity was born among the miners, bringing forth the idea of a strike that promised to challenge the very heart of the industry.

Guardians of the Land - In that atmosphere, thick with uncertainty, few understood the depth of the land they fought upon. Little did they know that the spriggans, ancient guardians of Cornwall's rolling hills and hidden valleys, were watching over them.

While many thought of spriggans as myths, fearsome figures that protected the land, they were benevolent beings who maintained the delicate balance between nature and humanity. Failing to heed their warnings could awaken something that mere human efforts would not quell.

A Night of Resolve - On a late June night, tension ignited in the local tavern as the miners gathered to voice their frustrations.

Overhead, lanterns flickered, illuminating tired faces torn with worry, determination, and rising rage. In the back corner, Julia, with the heart of a lion, stood up to speak. "We must unite, lads! If we don't strike, they'll own us! They will wear down our spirit until we are nothing but dust in these mines!"

Just as her words resonated through the room, a sudden chill swept in, and the door creaked open, revealing Mr Wren, the village storyteller and custodian of local folklore. His presence commanded respect, and the air thickened as he delivered his cautionary message. "Listen, lads. If you rouse the earth, what lies beneath will awaken. The spriggans may protect this land, but they are not forgiving to those who disrupt the peace."

Disregarding Warnings - This warning fell on deaf ears for many. Despite Mr Wren's ominous tale, dismissive jeers filled the room. "Pah!" one miner retorted. "What is a bunch of old wives' tales against a man's hunger? We must fight!" The chatter churned within them, buzzing with fervour weighed down by uncertainty of what was to come.

Strange Occurrences - As the miners embarked on their strike, strange and unsettling events unfolded. Shadows flickered in the moonlight, tools vanished as though spirited away, and eerie clay sculptures resembling the miners' weary faces emerged by the mine entrances. Whispers of the spriggans protecting their land became a chilling narrative, evolving in the hearts of the miners, a foreboding spectre looming just beyond the edges of their understanding, brewing with a fear of the unknown.

A Call to the Spirit - Amidst despair and uncertainty, Joseph and Julia ventured into the depths of the darkened earth, cautious and firm. Within the cavern filled with the scent of clay and history, the two stood in silence, listening for answers. "Do you hear that?" Joseph called into the void, a mix of hope and fear in his voice. "We're fighting for our lives!"

Through the shadows materialised the figure of a spriggan, ancient, and awe-inspiring, with eyes as deep as polished stones. "Courageous ones," it bellowed, its voice echoing like a distant thundercloud, "you disturb the earth, and you disturb me."

A Spirit's Wisdom - The spirit's eyes pinched with wisdom as it looked at them. Julia, ever the brave soul, stepped forward, her voice unwavering. "I plead with you, spirit, help us! We cannot live on promises alone. A bitter winter looms ahead. Will you assist us in holding our ground?"

The figure tilted its head, contemplating her words, "You speak of struggle, but do you not perceive? An unheeded mine, an undervalued life, those who labour among you possess worth far beyond clay." The spirit shared tales of the old days, revealing how the ancient Cornish miners had lived harmoniously with the land and the spirits, gaining respect and favour from both.

The Emergence of Understanding - What unfolded in that exchange was magic, a realisation that with unity came strength, and true power emerged from understanding and dialogue rather than confrontation. Julia and Joseph emerged from the darkness; their hearts rekindled with purpose.

Recognising their newfound clarity, they rallied their fellow miners; their strike was no longer fuelled by anger. They resolved to approach the mine owners with a bolstered spirit, seeking dialogue rather than discord. Respect, they vowed, was their only requirement, not just for their labour but for their very existence.

A Shift in Perspective - As weeks rolled into months, the enigmatic spriggans watched from the shadows, guiding dreams and igniting conversations within the cores of the miners. They whispered the importance of humility and coherence, unlocking a new model where conflict became collaboration. When the miners confronted the owners, they did so with a united front, their voices bringing a chorus of peace and respect.

A Step Toward Cooperation - With that, the tides turned. Faced not with fury but genuine concern and determination, the mine owners, realising their oversight, agreed to a meeting that could change lives, one born out of communication rather than destruction.

The song conveys themes of resignation and existential reflection. The repeated phrases "It's still the same" and "Nothing's changed" suggest certainty and perhaps stagnation in life. The metaphor of life as "just a game" implies that the struggles and triumphs people experience may ultimately be trivial or transient.

The invitation to "have a coffee" and "take a rest" creates an atmosphere of intimacy and comfort, contrasting with the weighty themes of truth and existence that follow. The line "no one listens to a word we say" touches on feelings of isolation and the futility of communication, echoing a common sentiment in contemporary society where voices can feel drowned out in the noise of daily life.

The lyrics urge gratitude in the face of adversity: "Thank your God that we're still alive." This moment of acknowledgement could indicate a glimmer of hope amidst the darker reflections, suggesting that recognising the fragility of existence can lead to a deeper appreciation for life itself.

Overall, the song captures a blend of melancholy and resilience, exploring the complexities of human life while navigating between disillusionment and gratitude. It invites listeners to reflect on their own experiences and perceptions of reality, ultimately questioning how we find meaning amidst the uncertainties and games of life.

Chapter 10

"Song 10 Narrative – An Gof"

An Gof: A Ballad of Valour and the Soul of Cornwall

Within the peaceful village of St Keverne, in the rugged landscape of the Lizard Peninsula, a legend came to life. Known as An Gof, he was Michael Joseph to those closest to him, a blacksmith whose hands bore the marks of years of hard work.

His resonant voice and hearty laughter reverberated through the narrow lanes, spreading joy and fellowship among the villagers. However, beneath this cheerful facade lay a simmering unhappiness.

The Burden of Oppression - The people of St Keverne were weary and burdened by oppressive taxes imposed by the crown and landowners. A sense of despair hung over them like a thick fog; from this darkness emerged Michael, a shining example of strength and leadership.

He did not swing a hammer; he crafted hope, sparking a flame within his fellow villagers that motivated them to stand up against their oppressors. Michael's inspiring words flew from his forge like the bright embers that flow out of his fiery forge, igniting a passionate resistance against what they considered unjust.

Rallying the People - As their dissatisfaction grew, the villagers rallied around An Gof, inspired by his keen passion and steadfast determination. When the moment arrived to challenge the authority, it was Michael they looked up to, his vibrant spirit and charisma promising unity. They organised a march to Bodmin, where the people suffered similarly under the same injustices, to unite with a local lawyer whose eloquent words matched their fervour. With arms wide open, he urged them, "This tax is an affront to our very liberty! Let us march to London, where the king lives, to air our grievances!"

The March to History - They commenced a journey that would etch their names in history for all ages to come. The rallying cries of the Cornish boomed like distant thunder as their ranks grew from 6,000 to an impressive 15,000. Farmers, labourers, and craftworkers mingled on the dusty roads, their hearts unified against oppression. Armed with pitchforks and tools of labour and a heartfelt sense of coalition and justice, they built a community bound by defiance and determination.

Harmony Turns to Chaos - Their march was an illustration of solidarity, each step resonating with beats of songs and laughter that reflected their common aspirations. However, reaching Taunton, this harmony gave way to chaos. What unfolded would unravel an unprecedented chapter in the lives of the Cornish. In a fit of fury and despair, some of the protestors had banded together, separated from the rest, to slay a royal tax collector, changing their course from protest and dialogue to rebellion and quarrel. This act marked the start of a fierce phase, where demands for justice mingled with cries of battle, each voice adding to their collective heartbeat.

The Capture of Michael - Amidst the upheaval, Michael Joseph evaded capture for a time, his spirit unyielding amidst the turmoil. Yet the situation shifted, and they seized him, taking him to the Tower, where execution was threatened. Even in this bleak moment, Michael's resolve remained unshaken as, for him, the plight of his people came above his own life.

A Lasting Legacy - Before the gallows, he proclaimed, "I shall have a name perpetual and fame permanent and immortal!" His words were far more than a parting utterance. They rang out like a battle cry, a vow of remembrance for generations to come.

His body displayed grim warnings against rebellion in the streets of London. The essence of An Gof was far from extinguished. It transformed into a powerful emblem knitted into the rich fabric of Cornish history.

The Enduring Spirit of Resistance - Their courage and sacrifice would go through the ages, immortalised in the hearts of their people, and celebrated in my tenth song that pays tribute to the unwavering spirit of resistance.

An Gof's legacy highlights a crucial truth: courage can inspire transformation, and pursuing justice binds communities across generations. His story serves as a profound reminder that the spirit of defiance endures in times of severe distress, reverberating through the valleys and villages of Cornwall, encouraging us all to advocate for what is right, even when faced with overwhelming, almost unwinnable, odds.

In Honor of An Gof - Remembering An Gof, the tenth song honours a legendary figure and reflects on the enduring strength of passionate, steadfast and defiant leadership in the battle against oppression.

Song 10 – "An Gof"

La la la la la la
La la la la la la
La la la la la la
I see your ghost I see your eyes
I hear your voice a battle cry
Love as if you were to die tomorrow
Love as if you were to live forever

La la la la la la
La la la la la la
La la la la la la

Perpetual name fame, you're immortal
I feel the pain deep in my soul, you're immortal, immortal
La la la la la la
La la la la la la
La la la la la la

Run, Henry, run, can you hear the Cornish drum
An Gof will be here in the morning
Run Henry run can you hear the Cornish drum
An Gof will be here in the morning

Scene 29 - The Flames of Dissent

The Calm Before the Storm - In a quaint village, between the jagged cliffs and the restless waters of Cornwall, there lived a blacksmith named An Gof. His strong, calloused hands shaped metal and the fates of those who sought his skill. Each strike of his hammer resonated through the narrow streets and vibrant markets, carrying tales of love, loss, courage, and sacrifice.

One chilly evening, as the sun sank beneath the horizon, An Gof found himself polishing a newly forged sword; it was a magnificent blade, sharp as his wit, with a hilt intricately designed to mimic the swirling patterns of the crashing waves below the cliffs of Cornwall. The sword felt ferocious and demanding, as if it were alive.

Whispers of Darkness - As the village readied itself for a festival honouring the sea gods, an undercurrent of unease began to grip the community. Whispers of a dark force rising beyond the cliffs spread through the village; an army bent on pillaging the coast. Once united, the villagers now voiced their fears of impending danger.

An Gof stepped outside to inhale the cool Cornish air after finishing his work; the moon cast a ghostly glow over the fields while the stars twinkled mischievously above as if guarding secrets from another world.

A Visit from the Past - Suddenly, a chill enveloped him, and he saw her before him, the ghost of a woman, her form shimmering like mist. Her deep, sorrowful eyes displayed a lost love. An Gof recognised her as Selina, his mother, who had perished in a terrible storm long ago. She had been the guiding light of his life, inspiring him to create beauty from the raw metal he shaped.

"An Gof," her voice came softly, like the murmuring tides. "Your heart is heavy with concern. A storm approaches, not only from the sea and the land but also within the hearts of men. You must prepare the village to fight for their lives and dreams."

The Call to Arms - Emotion surged within him. "But how can I confront this darkness?" An Gof asked, his voice trembling.

"Unleash the strength forged in the fires of your heart. Create weapons of not just metal but of hope and courage. Rally the villagers and instil in them the belief that they can withstand the storm," Selina urged, her form shimmering with urgency. Her words ignited a fire within him, and An Gof returned to his forge with a heart full of hope and ambition.

Throughout the night, he hammered iron like never before, pouring his sorrow and love into every strike and every beat. Each weapon he produced carried a fragment of his spirit, an indicator of resilience.

United We Stand - As dawn broke, the villagers gathered, drawn together by an unspoken call that none heard but all answered. An Gof stood before them, resolute. "Friends, listen! Shadows may loom over us, but united, we can withstand the flood. These weapons I have forged are not mere tools for battle but symbols of our unity and determination to protect what we cherish." Empowered by his intensity, the villagers took up arms fortified by metal and hope.

When the landowners approached, fierce combat erupted, and shouts of valour filled the air. The battle was a mighty one. The villagers fought as one, and An Gof fought alongside his comrades, his heart racing with the memory of his mother, guiding him through each step he took on the field.

A Mother's Memory - During the battle, he felt her presence rejuvenating his resolve with every breath. Each swing of his sword resonated with her wisdom and visions of a brighter tomorrow. He fought not just for the village but to honour her memory.

At last, the tide turned in favour of the villagers, and with one determined push, they forced the enemy to retreat beyond the cliffs. And just as the sun began to rise, although momentarily, the danger had been averted.

The Spirit's Final Whisper - As cheers erupted from the villagers, An Gof was enveloped by a warm glow. In that moment of victory, Selina's spirit manifested one final time. With a radiant smile that rivalled the sun's brilliance, she whispered, "You have forged a legacy, my son," before fading into the light and leaving An Gof with a heart full of contentment and purpose.

A Rising Tension - "Gather around!" An Gof's voice cut through the lingering whispers in the village. "This is merely the calm before the storm; the king and his army will come, larger and more formidable!" One by one, villagers emerged from the shadows, their faces curious and concerned. The flickering candlelight revealed their exhaustion, clothed in tattered fabrics smeared with dirt.

After the battle, An Gof remained deeply focused on his work. He paused to wipe the sweat from his brow, the forge's fiery glow accentuating his rugged, resolute features. "We have borne the heavy burden of the king's rule for far too long. Just today, the tax collector demanded more coins than we can afford. They see us as mere subjects, but we are the men and women of this land forged by sweat and sacrifice. We are the ones who cultivate the fields and fill the king's table and belly while we go hungry," he declared, his hammer resting but the fire of his passion ablaze within him.

Sparks of Rebellion - A murmur of agreement swept through the crowd as an elderly woman, wrapped in a shawl, stepped forward. "Aye, lad, I lost my last chicken to the taxes. They'll take my house next! We can't endure this any longer! What do you suggest we do?"

Inspired, An Gof felt a spark ignite within him. He had seen the streets become a cauldron of discontent. "We rise together!" he proclaimed, his voice ringing with a spirit that infused hope into the hearts of those around him. "We will not meet the tax collector with mere payments; we will confront him and demand justice. If they seek our blood, they will have to shed it!"

The Flame of Unity - The villagers began to stir, their whispers growing into shouts of support. Although weary, An Gof's words sparked courage buried in despair. Old faces hardened by toil and young ones untouched by years of struggle shared a common fire in their eyes. Women clutched their husbands' hands, and men nodded with conviction, their eyes alight with renewed determination.

The Gathering Storm - As the sun set and the first stars appeared in the gathering darkness, An Gof sensed a change in the crowd, a potent blend of fear and resolve evolving into something formidable. "For now, we will not strike against the king," he clarified. "Let us be wise. We will devise a plan. We shall come together, speak with one voice, and when the tax collector returns, we will demonstrate that our spirit cannot be subdued." A murmur of agreement rippled through the crowd, their unity turning the chill evening air into something warmer, charged with possibility.

The Voice of Concern - A young woman's voice pierced through the crowd. "But what if they send an army? What if they take us prisoner?" Her face was pale, and her hands trembled as she clutched the edge of her shawl.

An Gof met her gaze, recognising the fear she bore. "Let them come! If they think we will retreat into the shadows, they are mistaken. We have shown our unity and the courage that arises from desperation. Our lives have been stifled long enough. The world has forgotten our strength, but we will remind them. The king may wear a crown, but we are the roots of this kingdom! It's time we make our voices heard."

The Spark of Unity - As his words crackled with the intensity of forge fire, the villagers' fear evaporated, replaced by a shared understanding and an unbreakable bond. They resolved to a rally in the market square, calling upon their friends, family, and neighbours to join them in their stand against oppression. In that moment, An Gof's dream of unity became a living force, pulsing through the hearts of all who gathered.

Forging the Plan - As midnight approached, plans took shape. Villagers dispersed to gather supplies, some seeking banners, others collecting food, while a few enlisted the brave and young to join their cause. An Gof remained at the forge, shaping not just metal but also the indomitable spirit of those around him. The sound of the hammer's strike echoed in the quiet of the night, like the beating heart of the rebellion itself.

The Dawn of Defiance - As dawn broke, painting the landscape in hues of gold and crimson, An Gof stood in the square among the townsfolk, their faces determined. When the tax collector arrived, flanked by sentries meant to intimidate, he was met not with fearful silence but with a collective roar of defiance. The sun, now rising high above the hills, illuminated their faces, casting them in a fierce light that no soldier or tyrant could diminish.

Confrontation with the Tax Collector - "What is the meaning of this?" the tax collector demanded, but confused. "You dare defy the king's orders?"

An Gof stepped forward, his heart pounding like his hammer's rhythm. "We are not your slaves or shadows scavenging for scraps. We are the lifeblood of this land, and we demand justice! For too long, you have taken from us, and now you will hear us. We will not bear the burden of your demands without a voice or recourse!"

The Foundations Tremble - The tax collector's bravado faltered as the villagers closed ranks behind An Gof, and at that moment, the very foundations of the kingdom trembled. The united cries of the wronged surged through the air, flowing beyond the horizon, a sound that would reach the ears of the king himself, awakening long-dormant roots of rebellion.

A New Beginning - This marked not the conclusion but rather a fresh start. The seeds of transformation had taken root in the hearts of the Cornish people. The rebellion was no longer a mere spark but a wildfire, ready to spread beyond the hills to sweep across the land.

The Forest Gathering - Deep within the forest, a gathering was happening as An Gof approached. The air was thick with the scent of pine and earth, the shadows of the trees long and looming as if they, too, were watching, waiting for the next move.

Scene 30 - The Spirit of Collaboration

Within the forest, ancient tales whispered through the robust branches of trees entwined like long-time companions. As dusk descended, a diverse gathering of beings assembled, bound by a mission of great urgency.

The atmosphere crackled with anticipation, a symphony of converging voices, whispering leaves, and the distant calls of owls. The sky, painted in hues of lavender and gold, seemed to watch over them, a silent witness to the weight of the decisions being made below. Among spriggans, knockers, and humans, the vital necessity for collaboration loomed against an imminent threat: the king's advancing army.

At the forefront were the spriggans, the forest's guardians, standing no taller than two feet. Cloaked in earthy tones that mirrored their surroundings, their bark-like limbs shimmered in the fading light while their amber eyes sparkled with mischief and wisdom. They were the keepers of the forest's secrets, playful spirits adding life to the gathering.

Gerran, adorned with golden patterns on his skin, exuded authority; his centuries of wisdom and experience instilled confidence in those around him. With each word, he spoke as a leader and as the embodiment of the forest itself, his voice carrying the weight of ages past.

Next to Gerran stood Lowena, a human-spriggan hybrid. Her transformation into a spriggan reflected her commitment to her heritage and the cause. With wild curls and fierce green eyes that seemed to pulse with the forest's magic, she fostered a sense of camaraderie among her companions. In the embrace of the ancient trees, she felt the land's heartbeat, beauty, and pain intertwined with her spirit.

Then, there was Edmond, a disillusioned prince who sought a purpose beyond the gilded life of royalty. Yearning to right the wrongs inflicted by his lineage, he found solace among these misunderstood beings. With a heart scarred by the destruction caused by human greed, he pledged to fight for the land and its inhabitants, earning the respect of his new allies. His royal blood, once a symbol of privilege, now felt like a burden—a reminder of everything he sought to change.

Joining the assembly was Solomon, the captain of the "Sea Spirit." His weathered face bore the marks of years spent navigating the seas; his curiosity remained undiminished. His thoughts turned to the waves and storms threatening his maritime home and the forest.

He shared tales of nautical strategy, imparting wisdom from his seafaring adventures. His eyes, blue as the sea below, gleamed with a depth that could only come from a life lived on the edge of danger, where every decision could mean life or death. The group welcomed his insights, recognising the deep connection between the ocean and the forest, although they were worlds apart.

As the flickering flames danced in the gathering's midst, Charlotte stepped up, her vibrant voice cutting through the night's stillness. "We may come from different walks of life, but our goals are intertwined. Each story brings strength. Think of us as a forge, every individual a different metal contributing to a weapon forged for the greater good."

Edmond, standing a little ways from her, nodded, his brow furrowed in thought. "But how do we inspire our people? Many still believe the king's might is unchallengeable."

Lowena leaned forward, her wild curls catching the soft light. "We share our own stories and show them our resolve. Let them see that the legacy we fight for is worth more than any throne built on injustice."

Joseph, fists clenched at his sides, added, "It's not just about our survival; it's about reclaiming what is ours. Every uprooted tree, every scarred land, will serve as a reminder of what we've lost. We need to stand firm and show the king that he cannot erase us."

Rev. H. Booth-Coventry adjusted his glasses thoughtfully, "Indeed, and it's our spirit, united, that will resonate louder than any army's chant. We must cultivate a fire within the hearts of our community, one that fights against despair."

From the shadows, Solomon interjected, his voice rich with experience. "Let us also watch and learn from one another. The way of the sea has taught me that storms reveal the strength of the land. We adapt, we flow, and we stand our ground."

Matt, the storyteller, chuckled heartily, his trademark laughter infectious. "And let's not forget the old legends! They lived through struggles like ours, remember? They remind us that within every dark night, there's a dawn waiting to break. We will weave their tales into our fight."

Julia stepped closer, her gaze igniting with determination. "And every woman's voice counts. The fight for suffrage is this fight. When we empower those who've been silenced, we create an army of voices too powerful to be ignored."

Charlotte grinned, "There's elegance in our diversity. Every speck of chaos can become a symphony when mixed well. We are a living tapestry, and the king will find it harder to unravel than he imagines."

"Hear, hear!" Joseph called out, his fist raised high. "Together, we are not just a defence but a declaration of existence!"

As the murmur of agreement filled the clearing, their voices rose in a chorus. Each proclamation brought them closer, each declaration entwining their fates further. The ancient and wise trees seemed to lean in as though the very earth beneath their feet was listening. The fire around them flickered, reflecting the burgeoning hope nestled within their hearts.

The Owlman, high above, hooted softly before offering solemn words, "The shadows you fear can be your ally. Let knowledge and unity guide your steps into this unknown. Remember, it is in the darkest nights that we often find our stars."

As the gathering murmured with anticipation, Charlotte looked around, her eyes gleaming with determination. "We stand as one, don't we? Every story, every sacrifice, woven into our fight."

Lily chimed in, her voice full of energy, "Absolutely! This land is in our bones. We won't let anyone take it from us. I can feel the magic in the air, and it's urging us forward!"

Joseph nodded firmly, a slight frown creasing his brow. "I've plotted their movements. We must be strategic; we won't rely solely on strength. Our intellect can be our greatest weapon."

Julia stepped up, her fiery hair catching the fading light. "And let's not forget the spirit of our ancestors! Their courage fuels us! We're the continuation of their stories. We carry their dreams with us as we fight."

Sarah raised her fists, her voice strong. "And what about our dreams? We can't let the darkness snuff them out! Each dream is a beacon of hope!"

An Gof, the blacksmith, placed a comforting hand on Sarah's shoulder. "You're right, Sarah. We're not just fighting for our homes; we're fighting for our future! Our iron will forge a pathway toward freedom!"

Rev. Booth-Coventry, standing at the edge of the circle, spoke gently but powerfully. "Together, we create our own fate. Those who come to challenge us will see our unity as an unyielding shield against despair."

Matt, with his storyteller's charm, smiled, "Every tale I spin tonight will remind us of our potential. We are not only defenders; we are the narrators of our legacy. Let our history inspire our fight!"

Morgawr, still emerging from the waves, added her booming voice, "And with my power over the tides, I will ensure that our land stays protected. No ship will approach our shores without facing the fury of the sea!"

The spiritual mermaid echoed Morgawr's sentiment, her melodic voice weaving through the crowd. "The currents shall be our allies. I promise to guide Solomon and rally the creatures of the deep to our cause. Together, we are unstoppable!"

Charlotte lifted Lily's staff high, feeling the collective energy of the crowd surge around her. "Then let's prepare! We are the embodiment of courage and resilience, standing shoulder to shoulder. Whatever comes our way, we face it united, for Kernow!"

A resounding cheer broke out, igniting a spark in every heart present. It was as though the very earth, the sea, and the sky had joined in their call to arms. They stood together, an unbreakable chain forged in hope and determination, ready to face whatever lay ahead.

Days passed like storm clouds gathering on the horizon as they worked tirelessly, crafting traps and strategies along the rocky coastline. They spent nights dreaming of bravery and unity, floating ideas that combined their powers to form an unconquerable wall against impending danger.

As the twilight draped the land of Kernow, the air hung heavy with the anticipation of battle. A constellation of hopeful faces illuminated by the first stars gathered around a sacred oak at the heart of the village. Here, under its sprawling branches, the very essence of their homeland surged, a powerful reminder that they were intertwined together by more than blood and soil but by shared dreams, stories, and an unwavering spirit.

The night deepened, and as the armies of the king began their approach, the soldiers of Kernow readied themselves, inspired by the tales and legacies that had come before them. As dawn's light would soon paint the skies, their hearts burned with resolve, ignited by the knowledge that they were not alone. The spirits of their ancestors, of every creature, tree, and wave, surrounded them. The spirits of the past shielded them, bound in purpose and hopeful for the future.

And so, on the eve of battle, they stood firm against the tide of despair, the united front of Kernow ready to confront all that threatened their beloved homeland, determined to turn the darkness into dawn.

Scene 31 - The Battle Begins

As twilight deepened into the evening, the battlefield was cloaked in shadows, the air thick with anticipation. The noble humans stood resolute on one side, their armour glinting in the fading light. Charlotte's voice rang out like a clarion, inspiring her troops with words that stirred the heart and steeled the spirit.

Across the valley, the king's formidable massive forces outnumbering the allies tenfold, advanced in precise formations, their banners snapping in the breeze—a stark omen of the impending threat. Between the two armies, the spriggans moved gracefully, their forms resembling the trees they hailed from, embodying otherworldly strength and resolve under the leadership of Lowena, whose unique presence fused the realms, radiating power and compassion, a living bridge between the forest and the battlefield.

Nearby, Captain Solomon's ship, the "Sea Spirit," bobbed in shallow waters, its crew packed on deck, fixated on the unfolding drama ashore and waiting for their moment. "Stand strong, brothers and sisters!" Solomon's booming voice crashed with the waves, his weathered hands steadying the wheel. "We are the storm; we are the tide!"

As the last rays of sunlight surrendered to an indigo sky, Lowena's chant soared over the rumble of the approaching onslaught. Surrounded by her fellow spriggans with their hands raised to the heavens, she harnessed the land's essence. Brilliant green and gold leaves erupted from twisted branches while mystical currents swirled around them like serpents. The earth pulsated each blade of grass and stone aglow with shimmering light as ancient spirits stirred to life.

From below, a swift rustling heralded the arrival of the knockers, their tiny hands clutching the earth. Popping up through cracks and crevices, their glinting eyes scanned the battlefield with mischief. "Now, clever ones, let's surprise them!" cackled their leader, beckoning his kin toward the chaos above. Mischief ignited their hearts as they emerged from the earth's underbelly, wielding shovels and pickaxes, ever ready to disrupt the king's advance.

And then, the clash unfolded in earnest. The king's forces surged forward like a relentless tide, their shouts drowning out Lowena's melody. As swords met and shields clashed, Gerran found himself at the frontline, his inner fire fuelling each strike. He caught sight of Charlotte's fierce resolve as she fought through the crowd, inspiring her people, each swing of her sword a defiant battle cry.

It was Lowena who shifted the tide. Channelling her spirit, she leapt into the chaos; her enchanting presence released waves of energy flowers that erupted beneath her feet, their petals bursting like confetti, infused with magic that ensnared their enemies. Every movement summoned ancient spirits that sowed confusion and doubt amidst the advancing king's men, their ethereal forms hindering the king's men's advances.

"With the roots of the forest and the strength of the mountains," Lowena declared, her voice a fierce command, as she collaborated with the spirits to conjure thorny vines that erupted from the ground and gripped the enemy's feet. The soldiers stumbled and fell, disoriented by the chaos surrounding them.

Amid the chaos of battle, the knockers seized their moment. Dashing between humans and spriggans, they tossed dirt, stones, and laughter into the fray. Their playful trickery caused the king's soldiers to stutter in their advance, caught off guard by the unexpected barrage from below.

The battlefield was a whirling cyclone, fierce and unpredictable. Gerran danced through the melee, his sword a blur as he fought for the spriggans. In a fleeting moment, he found himself back-to-back with Charlotte, their eyes locking in mutual understanding. Together, they forged ahead, cutting a swath through the king's ranks.

"Keep fighting!" Charlotte urged, adrenaline surging through her veins. "We are the voices of the oppressed! We will not be consumed by fear!"

As the hours pressed on, thickened by sweat and determination, a new energy surged just as despair threatened to take hold. The knockers had executed their plan masterfully. Against the encroaching enemy, the earth seemed to rise in revolt. The king's soldiers tripped and stumbled, ensnared by magic and by the very ground beneath them.

In the heart of the battle, Lowena and Gerran locked eyes amid the commotion, and time momentarily froze, allowing them to savour the unbreakable bond formed in the crucible of conflict. With her spirit blazing like a beacon, Lowena lifted her hand, summoning the fury of the sky, storm clouds gathered, lightning slicing through the darkness—a demonstration of nature's might, a power they could wield together.

With a thunderous crescendo, the battle reached its peak. Fate was not a single thread but an intricate tapestry woven from the heart, sacrifice, and unity. In the throes of conflict, humans, spriggans, and knockers united, reshaping the battlefield as a bulwark against tyranny.

As the clamour of battle echoed, Charlotte and Gerran stood side by side, drawing strength from one another. Together, they surged into the fray, energized to repel the relentless advance of the king's forces. The tide began to turn. Each swing of Gerran's sword, each rallying cry from Charlotte, ignited hope in their defences, transforming the battlefield into a haze of bravery and defiance.

The king's soldiers faltered as the spriggans and their impish allies, the knockers, ramped up their attacks. With every move, the earth beneath the oppressors seemed to conspire against them, pulling them into the treacherous mud and ensnaring them in the thorny vines conjured by Lowena's will.

"Fight for freedom! Fight for one another!" Charlotte called, her voice strong as the battle raged on. With every soldier that fell and every shout of courage from their side, the morale of the king's army began to falter.

Then, a thunderous crack reverberated through the air as lightning struck, illuminating the battlefield as if it were noon. Fear on their faces, the king's forces wavered, caught between the brewing storm above and their dwindling courage.

"Now!" Lowena's voice pierced through the chaos, rising above the uproar. Seizing this crucial moment, Gerran charged forward, channelling the bonds of friendship and solidarity that had united them all as one. With all his might, he swung his sword, cutting through the enemy and instilling fear into their hearts.

It was in that instant that the true miracle occurred. The spriggans and the knocker kin united their powers, summoning roots and branches wrapping around the soldiers, binding them in an unbreakable living web. King's men were entangled in vines as if trapped in cobwebs.

With the tide shifting in their favour, Charlotte gathered her warriors and surged onward, her voice unwavering and commanding. "We fight not just for ourselves but for our future! Stand firm and remember what we are fighting for!"

The combined forces of nature and humanity roared against their adversaries, steadfast and unyielding. The battlefield transformed into a display of defiance as they pushed through the remnants of the king's land army, each battle cry reclaiming more than land: freedom.

But it wasn't over; the battle of Kernow took to the sea, an ocean of chaos and valour, where shadows matted with light in a fierce embrace. As the last sounds of the day faded into the whispers of dusk, a thick tension hung in the air, infused with ancient magic, heralding the inevitable showdown between hope and tyranny.

An Gof steadied himself, drawing strength from the memory of the forest battle. The roar of the surf crashing against the shores mingled with the heartbeats of the warriors around him, their faces glowing in the shimmering moonlight on the waves, creating a surreal beauty juxtaposed with the grim battle ahead.

The ground trembled as Morgawr, the humongous sea serpent, surged forth, her colossal frame breaking the surface in a dazzling display of scales embellished by the dripping water of the ocean.

She rose majestically, her body arching as she sang resonating notes that rolled across the waters, a battle hymn that echoed in the hearts of all present. An Gof's grip on his sword tightened, feeling the blade twang in tune with the ancient powers at play.

Beside him, the mermaid shimmered, her voice a hypnotic melody that melded with the ocean's rhythm. She summoned her kin from the depths, a swift, shimmering wave of life emerging.

Dolphins leapt gracefully, sea turtles glided purposefully, and schools of iridescent fish darted forward, all joining the resistance. They became unified with the human warriors, forging an unbreakable bond that transcended the divide of species, united in their mission to stand against the oppressive king.

Soaring above, the Owlman cut through the twilight, his dark silhouette a sign of wisdom casting guidance upon the warriors below. Each hoot provided insight into the next attack, forging a connection steeped in the shared spirit of their struggle.

The enemy, imposing and menacing on the coast and beaches, now sensed the storm brewing against them.

As the king's soldiers advanced, the cacophony of battle erupted into mayhem—steel clashed against steel, and the cries of warriors filled the air, blurring the lines between humanity and the ethereal as magical beings rallied alongside their allies. An Gof's blade, gleaming in the battle light, led the charge, each swing carrying the fervour of their cause, the full essence of the vow they had made to reclaim their homeland.

The king had his dark sorcery. From the shadows emerged monstrous trolls and phantoms conjured by wicked spells, their presence demoralising even the bravest. The ground shuddered with each heavy step of the trolls, and despair crept among the coalition. An Gof felt a flicker of doubt, an unsettling uncertainty gnawing at his resolve.

In the chaos, he remembered the wisdom of the Owlman, the calming song of the mermaid, and the indomitable spirit of Morgawr. With a fire igniting within him, he raised his voice above the noise, "We are more than mere soldiers— we embody the hope of our people! We fight for Kernow, for our homes, for our families!"

A swell of courage surged through the assembled forces, igniting their determination. With renewed vigour, An Gof elegantly and precisely struck down foes while the mermaid summoned waves that toppled the massive trolls.

Quickly, the tide of battle shifted. The Owlman returned from the sky, vigilant and sturdy beside An Gof, guiding arrows with remarkable accuracy, their paths dictated by his foresight; each success bolstered the momentum of the soldiers surged, forming an unstoppable force.

In the heart of the fray, as dusk transformed the world into shadows, An Gof pressed toward the king, whose opalescent armour glimmered—a mockery of hope. Clad in dark promises, the tyrant wielded a sinister blade, its edge steeped in the cries of those he'd conquered and massacred.

Undeterred, An Gof felt the essence of the land around him infuse strength into his being, his mother's prayers guiding his every step, the valour of his people brought poise to his intentions, and the love for his land kept him undaunted. He had decided to reciprocate the king's generosity in menace.

Their blades clashed, elemental energies colliding in bursts of light and sound. In that instant, An Gof tapped into the collective magic of the land, the sea, and the sky. The air hummed with anticipation, and the essence of every spirit embodied within him surged forth, a blazing brilliance that mended the broken hearts and rekindled the dying embers of resistance.

Seizing his chance, An Gof pushed forward, glinting sword aimed at the heart of tyranny. A colossal wave surged from Morgawr, crashing against the king's defences, disorienting them. An Gof seized the opportunity. With his sword made from the heart of a star fallen from the heavens, he surged forward; he could feel the energy of every soul that had suffered under the king's reign flow behind him, lending him strength. With a cry that resonated with the hopes of the fallen, he thrust the blade deep into the tyrant's heart, piercing the darkness that had long ensnared the land.

Time seemed to pause, the clash of steel and cries of war subsided, replaced by the noise of liberation. The blade shimmered and glowed, a beacon of hope that pierced the shroud of despair as celebration seemed imminent; the abrupt silence shattered into chaos once more.

With lightning quickness, an unseen archer loomed in the shadows. An arrow, slicked in venom and fuelled by vengeance, sailed through the air, finding its mark deep within An Gof's chest. The warrior gasped, the warmth of life ebbing away as he staggered back, his sword falling from his grip, the glow dimming in the encroaching dusk.

The king's features twisted in disbelief as the magic faltered and the dark thrall over the battlefield shattered. A silence blanketed the war-torn ground, the echoes of conflict replaced by the sounds of liberation.

Morgawr's fury transformed into unyielding grief as An Gof lay crumpled on the ground; she coiled protectively around him. She let out an endless, deafening roar.

Beneath the moon glow and over the tranquil tides, a new dawn ascended upon Kernow, its people united, its spirit indomitable.

Those who fought transformed the once desolate battlefield into a sacred ground, demonstrating their bravery. Waves of deliverance were beckoned forth by the song of the mermaid and their paths were guided by the Owlman. Their collective victory was not a battle won but the reclamation of a legacy, an everlasting promise that hope can rise, even from the depths of gloom.

With a final, unearthly scream, the king crumbled as his power drained into the soil of Kernow. As the magical forces converged, the ground reverberated with liberation, dissipating the darkness that had long drowned the realm. As the last remnants of the oppressor vanished, replaced by an overwhelming wave of jubilation and unity, the warriors raised their swords high.

As the people started cheering, their voices rose like the chorus of a world awakening. Morgawr retreated into the embrace of the sea, her duty fulfilled, while the mermaid shimmered beside the shores, a lasting reminder of the bond forged between worlds.

Unified, the allies stood, guardians of a renewed world. As the conflict fades, the moon rises, casting an eerie glow over the land. Against the backdrop of the once-mighty banners of oppression, the weary yet triumphant warriors raised their weapons high, their victory echoed by the cheers and laughter of spriggans and knockers. Together, Charlotte, Gerran, and Lowena stood tall.

The song evokes themes of love, mortality, and the quest for immortality through legacy and memory. The recurring phrase "La la la" gives it a whimsical yet haunting quality, perhaps suggesting the contrast between the lightness of life and the weight of deeper existential thoughts. The lines about seeing a ghost and hearing a battle cry hint at a connection with the past, blending personal reflection with historical or cultural references.

The notion of loving as if one were to die tomorrow juxtaposed with the idea of loving as if one were to live forever highlights the duality of human experience—it urges listeners to embrace the present while also contemplating the lasting impact of their actions and affections. The repeated phrase "you're immortal" signifies a longing for transcendence, suggesting that love and memory can grant an enduring legacy beyond physical existence.

Moreover, the references to "Run, Henry, run" and "An Gof" connect to historical events, alluding to the Cornish rebellion and the desire for freedom and recognition. This fusion of personal sentiment with collective memory creates a rich tapestry that invites listeners to reflect on their own lives and the legacies they wish to leave behind. Overall, the song balances the ephemeral nature of life with the quest for meaning and remembrance, making it both poignant and thought-provoking.

Chapter 11

"Song 11 Narrative – Time to Say Goodbye"

When It is Time to Say Goodbye: Embracing the Bittersweet

Embracing the Weight of Loss - Death is a profound and mysterious concept that often leaves us facing a whirlwind of emotions. When we first learn of a loved one's passing, a heavy shroud of grief envelops us, compelling us to confront the harsh, unavoidable reality of farewell. In these moments, the sense of loss we feel is deep and multifaceted, intertwined with memories, love, and sorrow.

The Intimacy of Farewell - The phrase "It's time to say goodbye" carries significant weight as we navigate this heart-wrenching passage. As death draws near, the act of closing a loved one's eyes becomes an intimate, albeit painful, ritual. In those final moments, we may yearn for just one more heartbeat, one more breath, a fleeting instant to cherish the presence that has brought us so much happiness. We often close our eyes, hoping to see their face in our memories, only to feel the darkness swallow our shared moments.

Cherished Memories - Memories of laughter and affection remain with us, lingering like whispers. The memory of their gentle breathing may still resonate within us, a soothing reminder of the grace they embodied amid this pain. We have come to understand that sometimes love means letting go. Accepting the hard truth that they are destined for something beyond this world can be incredibly difficult.

The Presence of Angels - As we stand by their side, we sense the nearness of angels, a melodic comfort that promises them peace and freedom. This moment, filled with despair and hope, often leaves us trembling as we grasp their hand, imploring them to hold on while knowing we must let them go. This internal struggle reveals vulnerability and a desire to keep them close, even as we acknowledge their departure.

The Search for Solace - The loss brings an array of unanswered questions, leading us to seek solace in the belief that only God understands the profound truth behind it all. We realise that love is a unique gift, and though it may bring pain, it liberates us. The unbreakable bond we shared remains despite the physical separation imposed by fate.

Stars of Memory - In the aftershock of saying goodbye, memories shine like stars across the night sky, each twinkling point a witness to the love and connection we cherished. These memories, from smiles to laughter, serve as our guiding light through the shadows of sorrow.

The Persistence of Love - While confronting the cruel reality of death is difficult, we find comfort in knowing that love persists, serving as our compass and reminding us that our connection endures. As we navigate the intensity of grief, we must learn to hold on as tightly as we would in those final moments. The silence of love can be overwhelming; it is within this quiet that we discover our hearts remain intertwined.

Celebrating Their Spirit - Through whispered prayers and cherished recollections, we celebrate their life, ensuring their spirit remains connected to our own. When the time arrives to say goodbye, we confront a paradox: the grief of loss with gratitude for the time we shared. Embracing this bittersweet complexity allows us to remember that love does not dissipate; it transforms, guiding us through our mourning.

The Promise of Memories - The strength we carry in our hearts ensures that, although their physical presence may fade, love will forever shine, illuminating our paths as we move forward without them. In summary, while we may bid farewell, every heartbeat and reflective moment honours their memory. It is not a true goodbye; it is a promise to cherish what was and to carry their love with us as we continue our journey.

A Dedication - I dedicate my eleventh song, "Time to Say Goodbye," to a close and treasured friend.

Song 11 – "Time to Say Goodbye"

I close your eyes, but you're not sleeping,
I can see your face.
I thought I heard you breathing,
With your amazing grace,
Looks like it's time to say goodbye,

Hold my hand, stop me from shaking,
I'll hold you close; I can't let you go.
I see the angels they are gathering,
They're getting close to your soul
Looks like it's time to say goodbye.

Only God can know the answer,
I know you loved him so,
Heaven has a gift now.
I've got to let you go.

Hold my hand, stop me from shaking,
I'll hold you close; I can't let you go.
I see the angels they are gathering,
They're getting close to your soul
Looks like it's time to say goodbye.

Hold my hand, stop me from shaking,
I'll hold you close; I can't let you go.
I see the angels they are gathering,
They're getting close to your soul, oh.
Looks like it's time to say goodbye.

Scene 32 - The Fall of An Gof

The Relentless Battle - As the relentless battle ended and night turned to day, the atmosphere sizzled with an almost tangible tension, one that only the most courageous warriors could withstand. Amid the war-ravaged terrain stood An Gof, a brave warrior renowned for his courage and strength, facing the relentless enemy advance. His presence shone as a beacon of hope for his fellow fighters, embodying their defiance against tyranny and personifying liberty. He was a symbol of all that was worth fighting for – freedom, justice, and the will to resist. However, fate had a different course in store for him that fateful night.

The Archer's Vengeance - From the shadows, the king's archer lay in wait, cloaked in darkness and as patient as a serpent ready to strike. His eyes, cold and unforgiving, narrowed with the weight of vengeance. With a swift motion fuelled by vengeance, he nocked an arrow tipped in deadly venom, a malicious potion designed for an instant and merciless kill. The bowstring sang through the dusk air; the arrow found its target with ruthless accuracy, embedding inside An Gof's chest. The poison spread like wildfire, quick and lethal.

The Mortal Blow - Time seemed to freeze as the warrior gasped, his steel-blue eyes widening in disbelief. The warmth of life faded, replaced by an icy inevitability. He staggered back, his trusted sword slipping from his grasp, its final clatter against the stones reverberated like a mournful tolling bell. A grim silence followed, the weight of his loss hanging heavy in the air, more suffocating than any battlefield clamour. The light of dawn cast an eerie glow on him, intensifying the tragedy of his fate. The shadows seemed to retreat as though the world held its breath in sorrow.

Silence on the Battlefield - Silence enveloped the battlefield, erasing the once-roaring sounds of clashing steel and battle cries, leaving an unsettling stillness that echoed the shifting fortunes of war. In the aftermath of violence, the emptiness was profound, like the world had momentarily forgotten how to move. In that silence, hope was eclipsed by sorrow. An Gof, who had fought for freedom and justice, now lay crumpled in the blood-soaked earth, a hero extinguished far too early.

Memories of Valor - As his life ebbed away, memories surged before him: moments of brotherhood with fellow warriors, laughter shared during scarce moments of peace, and the dreams of liberation that had fuelled his resolve. Each recollection served as a poignant reminder of his humanity amid the chaos of war. Amidst the remnants of conflict, his thoughts turned to his people—ones who relied on him for guidance and strength—now facing an uncertain future without their unwavering protector. Though growing colder with each passing second, his heart bled for them, for the struggle that would continue without him.

The Ripple of Grief - Grief morphed into a fierce anger in the hearts of those left behind. On that hallowed ground, marked by the sacrifices of innumerable souls, An Gof's death stood as a stark reminder of the fragility of life and the anomaly of fate. His fall was not just the loss of one man but the shattering of a dream, the end of an era.

A Call for Retribution - His comrades, witnessing his fall, felt a collective shudder weave through their ranks. The weight of their losses bore down on them, igniting a burning desire for retribution, not just against the archer concealed in darkness but against the very powers that had instigated this war.

The Spirit of Resistance - In his final moments, An Gof's spirit sparked a resilience among his comrades, provoking in them a fierce determination to honour his legacy through their actions. As dawn awoke, wrapping the battlefield in a cloak of light, his spirit whispered among them, urging them to resist despair and rise against their oppressors. His sacrifice was a flame that would never be extinguished.

A New Dawn - A new dawn awaited, borne from the pain of loss and vengeance. An Gof's sacrifice would resonate in the hearts of his comrades, serving as a catalyst for rebellion, fuelled by hope and an unyielding quest for justice. Though his body lay still, his legacy burned brightly in the hearts of those who remained. Although the archer in the shadows had struck true, An Gof's indomitable spirit would endure, echoing through the hearts of those he sought to protect, an unbreakable human spirit in the face of despair.

My song - "Time to Say Goodbye," captures the profound emotional turmoil that accompanies loss and farewell. Through its poignant lyrics, the song conveys a deep sense of love and longing amidst the inevitability of parting. The imagery of closing one's eyes yet still being able to see the beloved's face evokes a bittersweet remembrance, where the presence of the loved one lingers in memory even as they slip away. It is a painful yearning that grips the soul with the knowledge that a shared moment will never return.

The repetition of holding hands symbolises a desperate connection, an attempt to bridge the chasm created by impending separation. This act conveys vulnerability and a human instinct to seek comfort in the face of grief; it underscores the struggle between the desire to cling to life and the acceptance of mortality. In those final moments, the clasp of a hand can feel like an anchor to an already drifting soul. The mention of angels gathering adds a spiritual dimension, suggesting a transition from the earthly realm to a higher plane, which can bring both comfort and sorrow.

Furthermore, the lyrical acknowledgement that "only God can know the answer" reflects a deep yearning for understanding in the face of loss, an expression of faith intertwined with confusion. The song resonates profoundly with anyone who has experienced the loss of a loved one, as it articulates the universal experience of grief while offering a glimpse of hope through the concept of an eventual reunion beyond this life. A reunion that, though uncertain, promises solace for an aching heart.

In essence, "Time to Say Goodbye" is not merely a song about mourning but also a tribute to love's enduring power. It invites listeners to reflect on their connections and the inevitable cycles of existence, illuminating the delicate balance between holding on and letting go. The song reminds us of the beauty found in the holding and the letting go of the brief but precious dance of life and death.

Chapter 12

"Song 12 Narrative – I Wish I Could Fly"

Wings of Dreams

The Dream of Flight - I often wonder about the meaning of my childhood dreams, especially the ones where I soared through clouds, gliding effortlessly, soaring through the midnight blue sky with a carefree spirit. The sensation of wind tousling my hair and the sun warming my skin still lingers in my thoughts. Beneath it all, those dreams were not just for fun; they were murmurs of a deeper longing, a yearning that would follow me into the waking world, whispering of freedom and untold possibilities.

A Day of Promise - I remember the day, the sun dipping low on the horizon, casting ambers and golds across the sky like an artist's palette. My friends and I played in a field near my childhood home, our laughter piercing the stillness like the intense cries of eagles gliding high above. That day, we agreed we would learn to fly. A flight of fancy, perhaps, but at that moment, the idea felt so real, so tangible, as if within our grasp.

Whispers of a Song - Later that night, as I lay wrapped in my bed with the moon casting silvery shadows, the words of a song hummed in the back of my mind:

I wish I could fly,

I'd fly away with you…

As sleep took me, the dream unfolded, a familiar sanctuary where worries dissipate into the ether. The dreamscape ignited with specks of light like fireflies, and there I stood, on the edge of a cliff that seemed high. Below, a great abyss of swirling mist beckoned, daring me to leap. My heart raced, a mix of fear and exhilaration.

The Enigmatic Figure - "Take my hand," a voice called. I turned to find a figure cloaked in shadows, a presence I knew well yet couldn't place.

"Don't look down," the voice urged, and I felt a strange comfort at the command. "Take a good look around."

As I looked over the precipice, something magical happened. The wind rustled the trees, almost singing their song of freedom. I stepped back, taking in the vastness of the night sky, painted with stars so bright they seemed to wink at me. I could see the silhouette of eagles soaring, gliding on invisible currents, unencumbered by the ground below. That golden ember of hope rekindled something deep within me, and my fear transformed into pure determination.

The Leap of Faith - With a deep breath, I leapt. In that eternal moment, time stopped and twisted. The air whipped around me, cooling my cheeks, and the exhilaration buzzed like a thousand bees. For a heartbeat, I was weightless, no longer tethered to earthly chains. I could see my childhood friends below, faces aglow with admiration and bewilderment, but my focus was locked on the moon, shining like a beacon in the dark.

Awakening from the Dream - Then the pain jolted me awake. I sat up, breathless, eyes wide. The remnants of the dream clung to me like a morning mist that wasn't ready to fade. I pondered the figure, still unsure of its identity. Who had it been? A guardian? A dream-avatar? Something deeper churned within me, and I sensed that this was not just a fanciful flight but a deeper reckoning with who I was meant to become.

The Continuation of Dreams - Weeks passed, and my dreams continued to unfold like a mythical tapestry. Each night, I returned to that high cliff greeted by the enigmatic figure who guided me, merging imagination with bittersweet reality. I realised the dreams were not just about flying but about freedom, a longing to break away from the mundane and grasp something extraordinary.

Revelations in the Dream - Then, one night, the figure revealed itself. It whispered, "It's time you see." With that, it took my hand, and the rush of spirit coursed through me. This time, we were not alone. Amorphous shapes transformed into beings of light, surrounding us in a constellation of familiarity. They were my childhood friends, their laughter blending with the cool breeze, their faces shimmering like stars among the eagles.

"Show us what to do," I pleaded, my heart full and aching as they encircled me.

Together, we stepped forward and leapt into the layered ocean of night. This time, it was an actual flight, a dancing, soaring exploration gilded in the glow of stellar brilliance.

Embracing Freedom - In this ethereal realm, amidst the expanse of stars, we flew together, side by side. I realised we were no longer bound by the limits of gravity but united by shared dreams and unwavering support. This was what it meant to fly, to embrace freedom, and to carry those we loved along with us.

The Dawn After - I awoke with the soft light filtering through my window at dawn's warning. The shadows of the figure and my flying companions faded, but their essence was still pulsing within me, indelible marks left on my spirit. The echoes of our laughter filled my heart. I could almost touch the brightness of our shared experience.

Navigating the Challenges of Life - The following years moved on, the world around me swelling with challenges and joys, aiding me into becoming who I am meant to be. I grew while carrying the dreams of flight within me. The nocturnal escapades transformed into a guiding presence, helping me navigate life's treacherous paths.

Yet, on an ordinary evening, as I was caught in the turmoil of a night filled with uncertainties, I felt that longing resurface. I stood on the edge of a metaphorical cliff, facing an unsettling choice that had the power to shatter my carefully constructed home.

A Step into the Unknown - I closed my eyes, embracing that tuneful chorus, "Take my hand and don't look down."

And I remembered. I remembered the freedom I felt, the cherished bonds that united me with the fabric of my friendship we had weaved together. I took a step forward again, not into an abyss but into a vibrant future filled with infinite and transformative possibilities.

The Flight Beyond - That night, with courage in my spirit and the memory of dreams guiding me, I learned to fly not in the physical sense but through the undeniable power of connection, love, and shared hopes that makes us all human.

Even now, when the darkness threatens to encroach, I find myself standing at that cliff, dreaming of the skies, eagles soaring, and, always, the hand I can take in my dreams.

Song 12 – "I Wish I Could Fly"

I wish that I could fly.
I'd fly away with you.
I see you in my dreams.
And I show you what to do.

Take my hand
Don't look down
Take a good look around
And I'll see you in my dreams
I wish that I could fly
In a sky of midnight blue
I see you in my dreams
And I show you what to do

Take my hand
Don't look down
Take a good look around
And I'll see you in my dreams

Eagles in the sky
Flying side by side
Soaring oh so high

Take my hand
Don't look down
Take a good look around
And I'll see you in my dreams
And I'll see you in my dreams

eagles in the sky
Flying side by side
if there's something I can do
To make it all come true
Then tell me in my dreams
And I'll see you in my dreams

Scene 33 - The Whispering Forest

As the last rays of sunlight disappeared, I turned to Lowena, excitement bubbling within me. "Look at me, Lowena! I'm human now! We can explore your world together and go on thrilling adventures like never before."

But her expression dimmed, and I sensed a chasm opening between us. "But at what cost?" she replied, her voice barely above a whisper. She stepped back as if I had transformed into something other than myself. "You have forsaken the forest, leaving behind the very essence of what made you a guardian."

A wave of sorrow washed over me at her words. "I've left it behind, yes, but I can learn to find my way back. We can return together, and you can show me your world while I share my magic with you. We can be together still!"

Her emerald eyes glimmered in the fading light, but the joy I longed to see was absent. "Can you truly learn?" she asked, her voice thick with grief. "You're no longer just a spriggan in human form. You've become something different, and I'm afraid I don't understand it."

Just then, a distant sigh echoed through the woods, resonating like a call from the heart of the forest itself. I could almost hear my old friends whispering through the leaves, urging me to remember the magic I had lost. "I can't let go of you, Lowena," I said as desperation clawed at my heart. "I need to find my way back. I want to reclaim what I have lost, to become whole again."

She reached for my hands, pressing her forehead against mine for a moment that felt timeless. "If that is your desire," she finally said, a hint of determination sparking in her voice, "I will help you. Together, we'll seek the ancient paths beneath the twisted branches of the oldest trees. But you must remember my love," she continued, solemnly, "while you may seek harmony, the flesh can never fully contain the spirit of a tree. You must find balance within yourself, and only then will you be whole."

Empowered by her words, we moved deeper into the woods, searching for the wisdom of the elder trees, the silent watchers of time. Shadows thickened around us as if the forest were holding its breath in anticipation.

Eventually, we arrived at the heart of the woods, where the oldest tree loomed before us, its gnarled branches twisting in the fading light. Approaching it, I felt an electric pulse in the air, a vibration of energy that resonated with my very being.

"Ancient one, hear us!" I called out, my voice trembling. "I was once a spriggan, woven into the magic of nature. Now, standing before you as a mortal, I seek your guidance to reclaim my lost spirit."

The wind was hushed, and a profound voice reverberated through the leaves. "To reclaim what you've lost, you must honour both your magical beginnings and the lessons of your mortal experience. This path demands sacrifice, yet within the space between realms lies your answer."

As the voice faded, sunlight filtered through the branches, revealing a shimmering pool at the foot of the ancient tree. "Drink from this pool, and let the memories of who you were wash over you," the voice cautioned. "But be wary: the journey will bring trials."

Taking a deep breath, I knelt at the edge of the pool, glancing at the still water reflecting the sky. "Will you guide me, Lowena? Help me find the balance I need?"

Her grip tightened around my wrist, a solid anchor against my uncertainty. "I will always be here for you," she reassured me, her voice a blend of hope and determination.

Closing my eyes, I allowed the whispers of magic to wash over me, feeling the cool water envelop my hands—warmth flooded through me, igniting my spirit. The trees began to sing, their melody echoing the love of roots reborn and the heartbeat of the earth.

At that moment, clarity settled within me. I would forever walk the line between my two worlds, not solely spriggan or human, but a new creation—a delicate harmony of magic intertwined with the material, immortal and mortal, purposeful and free. As I opened my eyes, light swirled around us, merging with Lowena's laughter, igniting the spark of a new journey rich with love, sacrifice, and the promise of unity between our worlds.

Together, we would carve a fresh path, a story uniquely our own, filled with the laughter of the forest and the resonance of whispered dreams.

My song - "I Wish I Could Fly," captures the profound longing for freedom and connection, encapsulating the universal desire to break free from earthly constraints and soar into new heights with a loved one. The recurring imagery of flight serves as a powerful metaphor for aspiration and liberation, suggesting that true happiness comes from communion with another soul.

The repeated plea to take the hand of a beloved, paired with the encouragement to "not look down," evokes a sense of trust and companionship. The act of flying together symbolises not just physical elevation but also emotional transcendence. There is an intoxicating blend of hope and yearning that resonates deeply throughout the verses, especially in the line "I see you in my dreams," which implies that while physical separation may exist, the bond remains strong in the realm of dreams and aspirations.

The Imagery of "Eagles in the sky, Flying side by side" amplifies this sense of unity—these majestic birds symbolize strength, freedom, and the ability to rise above challenges. The song's insistence on seeing the loved one in dreams illustrates the power of imagination as a refuge, offering solace and the promise of better things to come.

Ultimately, the song encapsulates a bittersweet hope: while one may dream of flying away to achieve freedom and connection, it acknowledges the difficulties of achieving such desires in reality. The emotional impact leaves the listener contemplating their own dreams and aspirations, and the connections that drive them towards those heights. Overall, "I Wish I Could Fly" resonates as a beautiful ode to love, longing, and the innate desire to reach for the stars only together.

THE END